There Was Something About The Kiss, Brendan Thought.

Not the way Cassie tasted, cool and sweet and tempting. Not the way she melted into him, fitting so perfectly against him.

He moved away from her, breathing raggedly. "I don't know what made me do that. We're friends— unless I've screwed that up."

"You'll only do that if you tell me I'm a lousy kisser. Then I'll have to beat you over the head."

She should have done that to him a minute ago, Brendan thought. Knocked some sense into him. "I'd say on a scale from one to ten, your kissing rates—" he narrowed his eyes "—about a twenty."

Cassie smiled. "You've saved yourself from a terrible fate. For now."

Brendan wondered what fate would bring the next time they met. The next time, he might not be able to stop with a kiss....

Dear Reader,

Celebrate the rites of spring with six new passionate, powerful and provocative love stories from Silhouette Desire!

Reader favorite Anne Marie Winston's *Billionaire Bachelors: Stone*, our March MAN OF THE MONTH, is a classic marriage-of-convenience story, in which an overpowering attraction threatens a platonic arrangement. And don't miss the third title in Desire's glamorous in-line continuity DYNASTIES: THE CONNELLYS, *The Sheikh Takes a Bride* by Caroline Cross, as sparks fly between a sexy-as-sin sheikh and a feisty princess.

In *Wild About a Texan* by Jan Hudson, the heroine falls for a playboy millionaire with a dark secret. *Her Lone Star Protector* by Peggy Moreland continues the TEXAS CATTLEMAN'S CLUB: THE LAST BACHELOR series, as an unlikely love blossoms between a florist and a jaded private eye.

A night of passion produces major complications for a doctor and the social worker now carrying his child in *Dr. Destiny*, the final title in Kristi Gold's miniseries MARRYING AN M.D. And an ex-marine who discovers he's heir to a royal throne must choose between his kingdom and the woman he loves in Kathryn Jensen's *The Secret Prince*.

Kick back, relax and treat yourself to all six of these sexy new Desire romances!

Enjoy!

Joan Marlow Golan

Joan Marlow Golan
Senior Editor, Silhouette Desire

Please address questions and book requests to:
Silhouette Reader Service
U.S.: 3010 Walden Ave., P.O. Box 1325, Buffalo, NY 14269
Canadian: P.O. Box 609, Fort Erie, Ont. L2A 5X3

Dr. Destiny
KRISTI GOLD

Published by Silhouette Books
America's Publisher of Contemporary Romance

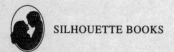 SILHOUETTE BOOKS

ISBN 0-373-76427-8

DR. DESTINY

Copyright © 2002 by Kristi Goldberg

This edition published by arrangement with Harlequin Books S.A.

Visit Silhouette at www.eHarlequin.com

Printed in U.S.A.

KRISTI GOLD

began her romance-writing career at the tender age of twelve, when she and her sister spun romantic yarns involving a childhood friend and a popular talk-show host. Since that time, she's given up celebrity heroes for her favorite types of men, doctors and cowboys, as her husband is both. An avid sports fan, she attends football and baseball games in her spare time. She resides on a small ranch in central Texas with her three children and retired neurosurgeon husband, along with various livestock ranging from Texas longhorn cattle to spoiled yet talented equines. At one time she competed in regional and national Appaloosa horse shows as a nonpro, but she gave up riding for writing and turned the "reins" over to her youngest daughter. She attributes much of her success to her sister, Kim, who encouraged her in her writing, even during the tough times. When she's not in her office writing her current book, she's dreaming about it. Readers may contact Kristi at P.O. Box 11292, Robinson, TX 76116.

To my mom, Jean, a heroine in her own right.

One

Adonis disguised as a doctor, and he was standing at Cassandra Allen's office door.

Cassie gave all her attention to Brendan O'Connor as he strode into the room, pulled back a chair and collapsed onto it. His ruffled brown hair indicated he'd had a hectic day. So did his eyes, a rich green-blue to match his scrubs. They changed like a chameleon to suit his attire, and sometimes to suit his mood. He *was* a chameleon, although most would not believe that of the calm, collected miracle worker. But Cassie knew better.

Even though she considered Brendan a good friend and an expert neonatologist, Cassie couldn't ignore her awareness of the man. Most women who came in contact with the doctor couldn't help but fall a little bit in love with him. She was no exception.

Flipping the case file closed, Cassie tapped her pen on the desk and said with mock exasperation, "Okay, so what did I do that brought you all the way down here?"

His slow grin caused Cassie's heartbeat to accelerate. "Nothing wrong. Just wanted to tell you how well I thought you handled the Kinsey couple today."

Cassie shrugged off the compliment. "That's what social work's all about. Besides, they're nice kids."

His smile faded. "Kids having kids. Give 'em a six-pack of beer and a case of hormones then look what happens. Premature twins."

She took a sip of too-cold, too-strong coffee and winced. Bad stuff, but the only thing she had available at the moment to wet her dry mouth. "At least the Kinseys have a good support system." And at least the new babies had two parents who seemed to love them, something Cassie had never really known. "No money to speak of, but I'm working on that."

"No high school diploma, either." Scooting back the chair, Brendan propped his heels on the edge of the desk, crossed his ankles and laced his hands on his abdomen. "I make these sick babies well, then I send them home to God-only-knows-what."

Cassie had known Brendan on a personal level for over six months now, had worked with him on several cases as one of San Antonio Memorial's staff social workers, yet she had rarely heard him criticize his patients' parents.

Although he was incredibly hard to read at times, she had gotten good at sensing when something bothered him. And this evening, something was bothering him. Badly. "What's really the problem, Brendan?"

His gaze zipped from his folded hands to her. "What do you mean?"

"Come on. It's me you're talking to. Cassie the clairvoyant, remember?" She smiled at the label he had personally given her when she'd accurately assessed his frame of mind on more than one occasion. Lately he hadn't even tried to hide his feelings, perhaps because he'd grown comfortable with her. Exactly what friendship was all about, and Cassie valued his friendship more each passing day.

She allowed him a few moments of silence. With Brendan, she had learned not to push. Eventually he would come clean without any persuasion on her part, if luck prevailed.

His sigh came out rough, frustrated. A hint of sadness passed over his expression, clouding his eyes. "I don't think the Neely baby's going to make it."

Cassie struggled for something consoling to say. Something that might lessen his pain. "Mrs. Neely delivered at what, twenty-nine weeks?"

"Twenty-seven. The baby's a little over two pounds with too many problems." He sat in silence for a few moments, his torment almost palpable. "Sometimes I wonder why I do this."

So did Cassie, but Brendan had never been forthcoming with that information. It wasn't the first time she'd seen him worried about one of his patients. In fact, it troubled Cassie that at times he seemed to worry too much. Not that he readily revealed his concern.

Despite the stress, something drove him. Some-thing personal, she suspected. She had never asked, and he'd never even hinted at his reasons for sub-jecting himself to such a high-pressure field.

"You do this because you're wonderful at it," she said in her optimistic voice. "You do it because you're the best."

"So you say."

"So I know."

"I do have some good news," he said.

Cassie leaned forward with interest. "You found the girl of your dreams?"

He hinted at another smile. "Matthew Granger's going home with his parents tomorrow."

She wanted to shout with relief, not only because the Granger baby had survived his premature birth, but also because Brendan hadn't found his life part-ner. That shouldn't concern her in the least. From the moment they'd met six months ago, she'd known they were destined to be only friends, though at times she found herself wishing for more. But Brendan had made it more than clear he wasn't looking for anything beyond friendship, and she cer-tainly didn't intend to complicate their relationship by making her feelings known.

"Wow, Brendan, that's great," she said. "Dr. Granger and Brooke must be thrilled. You need to concentrate on that. You're responsible for that little miracle, and so many others."

"Losing even one isn't good enough for me." He dropped his feet from the table and stood. "I'm get-ting out of here. I've had about all of this place I can stand."

One thing Cassie knew for certain, he didn't need

to be alone tonight, considering his present state of mind. And what did she have to go home to? An empty house and a cocky cat. Not at all appealing at the moment. Not when compared to spending the evening with Brendan O'Connor in some friendly competition.

All she could do was make the offer and hope that he accepted. "So you're through for the day?"

Brendan paused at the door. "Yeah. My shift's up. Segovia's taking over."

"Good. Meet me at the tennis courts in an hour."

He checked his watch. "It's late."

"We've played later than this before."

"I'm not sure what kind of company I'd be."

Time to bring out the big guns. Brendan was as driven as Cassie when it came not only to work but also to sports. She would shamelessly use that to her advantage, or at least try. "Nothing like a friendly game to alleviate stress."

"Thanks for the offer, but I'm not in the mood."

"Come on, Brendan. Be fair. It's my turn to kick your cute butt."

His expression softened and the familiar competitive gleam flashed in his eyes. "You think you can kick my butt, huh?"

"Yep."

"So you say."

"So I know." She rose from her chair and smiled. "And your answer is?"

He let go an exaggerated sigh. "I guess if you're determined to kick some butt, it might as well be mine."

"Great." She sauntered over to him and patted

his whisker-shaded jaw. "You might want to wear extra padding in order to protect your derriere."

"That's not necessary. You're not going to win."

"Whatever you say, Doctor."

His smile reappeared, deeper this time, revealing the prominent right-sided dimple creasing his cheek. She loved his smile. Loved it when he let down his guard and morphed from doctor to man. Loved it when he laughed, which didn't happen too often lately.

That would be Cassie's goal for the evening. To make Brendan O'Connor laugh—and, of course, to win.

"I won! I won! I won!"

Brendan stood at the net and chuckled as he eyed Cassie strutting around the court, racket held above her head as if it were a Wimbledon trophy. Her short white tennis skirt bobbed up and down with her revelry, revealing a nice glimpse of tanned thigh. A few strands of her shoulder-length silky blond hair escaped her ponytail and ruffled in the cool October breeze. That effervescent smile, those mischievous dark eyes, that prime athlete's body, could disintegrate any man's resistance. Even Brendan's.

But he wouldn't spoil their relationship by considering anything other than friendship, no matter how tempting she could be. He also wouldn't spoil her moment of victory by telling her that he had let her win. Okay, not exactly let her, but his heart hadn't been in the game. Considering what the next day would bring—the anniversary of an event he would just as soon forget—he had his mind on little else. He hadn't been able to forget, even after years of trying.

Cassie rushed to the net and taunted him some more. "I told you your butt was in trouble, didn't I?"

"Would you just leave my butt out of this?" He tried to sound serious, but he couldn't stifle more laughter or resist her joy.

She pointed and grinned. "Aha! You did it twice in one day."

"What?"

"Laughed."

He shrugged. "So? Are you keeping score?"

"Yes, and as promised, I did what I set out to do." She reached over the net and gave him a hefty slap on the part of his anatomy in question.

"You've really done it now, Cassandra Allen."

Brendan scaled the net but Cassie was too quick. By the time they'd made it to the commons area near the club's rear entrance, he'd caught up to her. He grabbed her around the waist and spun her several times, then turned her into his arms and held on fast.

"Let me go, Brendan O'Connor." She sounded winded, but not all that threatening.

"Not until you apologize for taking advantage of my exhaustion, and my vulnerable buttocks."

She jutted out her chin in determination. "Bully."

He tightened his hold on her and grinned. "*I'm* the bully?"

"I mean it. Let me go." Amusement flickered in her dark eyes as she wriggled against him.

He wished she would stop squirming. Parts of his body were finding it difficult to ignore her. Difficult to disregard her breasts pressed against his, her bare thighs touching his. All he had to do was release her, but for some reason he couldn't. Or maybe he didn't want to. "What are you going to do now?"

She stared for a moment, then a devious grin appeared. "You really want to know?"

"Yeah."

"Okay. You asked for it."

Working her arms from his grasp, she framed his jaws between her palms and kissed him square on the mouth.

Shocked, Brendan dropped his arms from around her.

She stepped back and smiled. "Works every time."

Brendan didn't move, didn't speak. He couldn't. His feet were fettered to the grass by some immovable force created by Cassie's lips. As far as kisses went, he'd rank it as harmless. But what it had done to him would qualify as anything but harmless.

Cassie pivoted on her tennis shoes and swayed toward the glass door. Brendan found his footing and followed.

She stopped with fingers poised on the handle and faced him. "I'm hitting the showers. Meet me in twenty minutes out front. You can buy me a beer."

Brendan needed to go home, get some shut-eye— 5:00 a.m. would come all too soon. But considering Cassie's impromptu kiss, he doubted he would immediately fall asleep. Might as well accept her offer. "Okay, you're on. But hurry."

"You hurry." With that she was gone.

He headed into the locker room and stood in the shower longer than usual, all the while trying to stop thinking about Cassie's kiss. All the while trying to figure out why something so innocent had him contemplating some not-so-innocent ideas.

After leaving the shower, he paused from drying off to tap his forehead against the cold locker door, attempting to dislodge the thoughts from his brain. It didn't work. He couldn't get the image of Cassie's kiss out of his head. Why had she done it? If she'd really wanted him to let her go, she could've punched him. Actually, he'd reacted as if she had. Maybe she'd intended to shake him up. If that had been her goal, she had definitely succeeded.

But he liked Cassie a lot. Liked the fact she was a great listener, a compassionate friend. He didn't intend to mess up a good thing by doing something stupid like kissing her back. Really kissing her.

He didn't need any complications right now. His job was complicated enough. So was his life.

Brendan dressed in jeans and T-shirt then set out to find Cassie. He came upon her at the front doors impatiently tapping her foot. "You're five minutes late," she said.

"The showers were crowded." A blatant lie. Only one other guy was in the shower, and he'd finished long before Brendan had. Cassie's spontaneous kiss had kept Brendan under the spray longer than planned, but he didn't intend to make that admission. Best to just ignore it, if he could. Maybe a beer would help. Maybe a sudden bout of blindness might, too.

They walked to the small lounge down the street and took their favorite table in the corner. The place was practically deserted with only a couple of businessmen seated at the bar, nursing their drinks and talking about their latest ventures.

Brendan ordered him and Cassie a beer, a routine that had become as welcome and familiar as her smile. He liked import; she favored domestic. He usually drank two; she rarely finished one. He smiled to himself when he considered how he had memorized her habits—the way she always swept her hair back with one hand, her high-energy aura, the fact that she always toyed with whatever was in reach, be it a straw or paperclip. Tonight was no exception. Right then she was steadily shredding a cocktail napkin.

Brendan began the conversation with a belated apology. "I'm sorry I came down so hard on the Kinseys."

Cassie stopped her shredding and laid a palm on his hand where it rested on the table. "It's okay, Brendan. Really."

"No, it's not okay. I don't have any right to judge anyone." His statement held more truth than Cassie would ever know.

Pulling his hand from beneath hers, he picked up his beer to thumb away a drop of condensation on the mug, wishing he could as easily discard his unexpected reaction to Cassie's touch. Being so close to her had never bothered him before. But it bothered him now in a very elemental way.

He'd never required more from her than easy conversation. He sure as hell hadn't *needed* to touch her, although many times he had wanted to. Right now it was all he could do to keep his hands to himself, resist the urge to trace the contours of her mouth with a fingertip, with his own mouth.

He tried to shake off the sudden urges, but they wouldn't go away.

She took up the paper-mincing where she'd left off. "You're frustrated and concerned about the pitfalls of teen pregnancy, Brendan. No one can fault you for that."

No, Cassie wouldn't fault him now. But if she ever found out that his reaction to the young parents had to do with his own lack of judgment years ago, she might change her mind. "At least they're trying, I guess." More than he had ever done.

Cassie sipped at her near full beer and regarded him with concern. "True. They both seem committed to raising their babies. Heaven knows that's not always the case."

Brendan imagined she had seen it all as a social worker. The good and the ugly. He admired her conviction, her strength. If only he had been so strong, then and now. For a moment he thought about confessing his sins to Cassie but reconsidered. She didn't need to know about his lousy past mistakes. That could very well lower her opinion of him, and ruin the best friendship he'd ever had.

He glanced at the clock flashing an ad for premium scotch—11:00 p.m. Later than he'd realized. He definitely needed to head home. As bad as he hated to leave Cassie's company, he had a responsibility to his patients to be at his best come morning. "Are you done?"

Cassie seemed to have zoned out, carried off into some realm of consciousness that didn't include him. Totally out of character for her. Normally she was always attentive. Maybe something was disturbing her, too.

He waved his hands in front of her eyes. "You in there?"

Startled, she brought her attention back to him. "Sorry. Just daydreaming, I guess." She smiled, a shaky one. Her dark eyes looked troubled. "Are you ready to leave?"

"Not until you tell me what's wrong."

She gripped her near-full mug with both hands. "Nothing's wrong. I was just thinking, that's all."

"About what?"

"About babies."

That definitely threw him mentally off-kilter. "Is there something you want to tell me?"

"Like what?"

"Are you pregnant?"

Her eyes widened. "Are you crazy?"

He shrugged. "You're a beautiful woman, Cassie. Anything's possible."

"You're so wrong, Dr. O'Connor. One would have to be—how should I say it—exposed in order to be expecting. And unless I slept through it, that hasn't happened in a long time."

"No prospects?"

"No way."

"Why is that?" he asked, genuinely curious.

"Why is what?"

"Why haven't you settled down? As long as I've known you, I don't remember you ever mentioning dating anyone."

She shrugged. "I don't have time for that right now. My work is too hectic. Besides, I don't intend to settle down or have children until I have all the time in the world to devote to them."

That relieved Brendan, especially the part about

her not having any prospects to father her offspring. Although he had no say in what she did, or whom she did it with, he didn't like the thought of Cassie carrying on with some guy that he knew nothing about. "Well, heck, Cassie, your lack of exposure is really a shame. Anything I can do about that?"

She crumpled the napkin's remains and tossed the wad at him. "You're so funny."

Truth was, he wasn't necessarily being funny. He didn't want any kids, either, but practicing with Cassie wasn't at all repulsive. In fact, it was a downright pleasant idea. One he had no business entertaining.

He yanked back his chair and stood. "Time for bed." Man, oh, man, he hadn't meant to say that.

If Cassie was at all shocked, she didn't show it. Instead she grinned. "Brendan, as much as I'd love to go to bed with you, I'm thinking maybe we should pick a time when we're not quite so tired from work and our tennis game."

Was she kidding? Did she really want to go to bed with him? Nah. As usual she was trying to get to him with her sassy sarcasm. Two could definitely play that particular game.

Leaning forward, he braced his hands on the arms of her chair. "You're right, Cassie. If I'm going to show you all the O'Connor moves, that's going to require all night. As it stands, I've got a NICU full of preemies that need my attention, and I need to be fully awake in the morning."

Cassie slipped her bag over her shoulder and gave a one-handed sweep of her hair. "All night, huh? It would take me all of ten minutes to bring you to your knees."

Blood rushed to Brendan's ears, along with other

places much lower. He took a step back and allowed her to stand. But her sensual challenge echoed in his brain. Ten minutes? No way. Then again, she could be right. At the moment, his knees felt like putty, and it wasn't from the effects of the tennis game or the lone beer.

Brendan walked Cassie to her car thinking he should see her off and get out of there fast, before he made one huge mistake. Before he suggested that he had a few more minutes to spare. Ten minutes, to be exact. He chalked up his sudden desire to stress, his recent lack of sex. Maybe even the need for escape from life's realities. The need to forget past mistakes. By virtue of her presence, Cassie happened to be on the receiving end of that need, or she would be if he didn't get the hell out of there.

When they reached her faded red sedan, she turned to him once again. "Good game, O'Connor. And I promise I'll go easier on you next time, in deference to your demanding profession and your poor tired bootie."

He didn't want her to go easier on him. He didn't want her to leave, either. Right now what he wanted and what he needed had little to do with competition and a whole lot to do with flawed judgment. "I had a great time, too, except for one thing."

"My gloating?"

Without regard to wisdom, he cupped her jaw in his palm and stroked a thumb down her silky cheek. "It has to do with something you started but didn't finish."

"Well my gosh, Brendan. I'll pay you back for the beer. Besides, you're the one who rushed me—"

He cut off her words with a kiss. Not a simple

innocuous peck. There was nothing innocent about it—not when her lips parted—or the way he took advantage of the moment and slipped his tongue inside the warm heat of her feisty mouth. Not with the way she tasted, like the peppermint she'd grabbed on the way out of the bar, cool and sweet and tempting. Definitely not the way she melted into him and fitted so perfectly against him.

But perfection had a price. Brendan's body was paying it. He was just this side of losing control. He couldn't allow that any more than he could allow the kiss to continue. Not at the expense of their friendship.

He moved away and issued another apology on a ragged breath. "I don't know what made me do that."

She leaned back against the car and folded her arms beneath her breasts. Her cheeks were splotched with red, her eyes dark and dazed. "I'm not sure what good grace dictates at this particular moment, but all I have to say is let's not make a big deal out of this."

Brendan grabbed his nape with both hands thinking he should probably wring his own neck for being so stupid. "It is a big deal."

She inclined her head and studied him straight on. "Does it really have to be? I mean, it's not like you threw me to the ground and ravished me."

It's not like he hadn't considered that, either. "We have a great friendship going here. Or we did. Unless I've screwed that up now."

"The only way you'll do that is if you suddenly declare I'm a lousy kisser. Then I'll have to beat you over the head with my racket."

She should have done that to him a few minutes ago, Brendan decided. Knocked some sense into him. "As far as your kissing ability is concerned, I'd say on a scale from one to ten you would rate…" He narrowed his eyes and studied her.

"I'm waiting."

"About a twenty."

Cassie's spirited smile jump-started Brendan's pulse back to life. "Lucky for you, you've saved yourself from a terrible fate. For now."

Brendan wondered what fate held in store for them the next time they met. If he didn't get a grip, next time he might not be able to stop with only one kiss.

Two

A rough tongue abrading Cassie's cheek woke her with a start. She opened her eyes to a gray furry feline curled up on her chest eyeing her expectantly.

A sudden sense that something wasn't quite right niggled at her muddled mind. Then she remembered. Brendan's kiss. The no-big-deal kiss. What a joke. Even though she'd said otherwise, it had been a big deal. It still was.

She rested one hand on the cat's head and the other over her eyes. While she scratched the tabby behind his ears, she relived every moment of the kiss in feature-film clarity—the soft feel of Brendan's lips, the silken glide of his tongue, the strong yet careful way he had held her. She shouldn't be surprised that he'd kissed her with the same gentleness he practiced with his tiny patients. She *should* be surprised that she had so actively participated and so willingly enjoyed it.

No matter how hard she tried, she couldn't fathom what had happened between her and Brendan. A momentary lapse in sanity? A glimmer of chemistry? A mutual need?

All of the above?

She couldn't let that happen. Long ago she had learned that intimacy did not lead to love. At one time she had made that mistake only to learn that giving in to physical needs only led to heartache. Giving all of yourself to someone didn't mean that that someone would give themselves emotionally to you.

Cassie uncovered her eyes and checked the bed-side clock. Although it wasn't quite time for her to get up, she might as well since the hungry cat and thoughts of Brendan's kiss wouldn't let her go back to sleep.

"Okay, Mister. Time for tuna."

She picked up the cat, who gave a meow of protest and a nice love scratch down Cassie's neck as she carried him into the kitchen to feed him. She opted for a diet soda instead of coffee after doling out disgusting kitty tuna. Then she went into the bathroom and began applying her makeup only to poke herself in the eye with the mascara wand when she couldn't keep her mind on what she was doing.

Now she was an absolute mess—bloodshot eyes, a red welt compliments of the kitty, and too-fine hair that refused to do anything but lie flat against her head.

She added drops to her eyes before applying her contacts, tried to hide the unsightly scratch with a turtleneck and twisted her uncooperative coif up into a plastic clip, sprigs of hair sticking out on top of her head like random wheat.

Cassie feared this was only the beginning of a daylong battle for control with Brendan invading her brain. How was she going to face him? Like a mature adult, of course. The spontaneous kiss would ruin the relationship only if she let it. She wouldn't do that. Brendan's friendship meant too much to her. Neither of them wanted to take the relationship to another level. Or did they?

As Cassie climbed into her car and headed for the hospital, she wondered whether that kiss was only the beginning of something more. Something unexpected and maybe even welcome. Maybe even something wonderful.

"Cassie, you've got to come see him!"

Cassie turned from the In box on her file cabinet and regarded her unexpected visitor. Michelle Lewis Kempner stood at the office door, all smiles and elation, not a strand of shimmering dark hair out of place, her makeup applied to perfection.

Cassie felt like road kill in Michelle's presence. "I've already seen your husband. Passed him twice this morning as a matter of fact."

Michelle rolled her blue eyes. "Not him, silly. My new nephew. He's all dressed and ready to go home. Hurry before Jared and Brooke leave."

Cassie suddenly remembered Brendan telling her that the Granger baby was going home. Not surprising she had forgotten that bit of welcome news considering the events from last night. She certainly didn't want to miss seeing the family off. But if she followed Michelle up to the fifth floor neonatology ICU, chances were she would run into Brendan. Maybe that wouldn't be so bad. After all, the entire Lewis clan would be there, the attention focused on the Granger baby. A good place to get lost in the crowd. Besides, she enjoyed being around the close-knit family even if the matriarch, Jeanie Lewis, was a bit on the flighty side. At least Michelle and Brooke had a mother, despite her flaws.

Cassie did want to see little Matthew Granger finally free from the constraints of IVs and other equipment that had brought him to this moment. If Brendan happened to be there, she would simply deal with it.

"Okay, give me a second." For some reason Cassie felt the need to do a quick touch-up. She pulled a mirror and a tube of lipstick from her desk drawer. Unfortunately, her hair looked like the product of a screwdriver rammed into an electrical outlet. Not much she could do about it now.

"Hurry up, Cassie."

Cassie shoved the drawer closed on the reminders of her bad-hair day and followed Michelle out the door. Michelle's husband, Dr. Nick Kempner, joined them on the elevator along with two teenage girls.

"Hey, where have you been all my life, beautiful?" Nick gave his smile and a kiss to Michelle. The girls giggled; Cassie grinned. She couldn't help it. The couple's joy over seeing each other was contagious, serving as fuel for Cassie's fantasy that someday she might be as lucky as Michelle.

The elevator seemed too small to contain Michelle's overt enthusiasm. She rocked back and forth on her heels and muttered, "This thing is so slow."

"They'll wait for you, Auntie Michelle," Nick teased.

"I know. But I can't wait to get my hands on him."

After the teens exited on the second floor, leaving only Cassie and the Kempners, Cassie regarded Michelle with a curious stare. "Are you getting some maternal urges, Michelle?"

Michelle and Nick exchanged a look. "I have some urges all right," Nick said. "Cassie, mind getting off on three and walking up to five? I was thinking maybe I'd take advantage of my wife in this empty elevator."

Michelle sent him a playful look. "Nick, we just got back from our honeymoon yesterday." She turned her grin on Cassie. "The man is greedy."

A bite of envy mixed with embarrassment fired up Cassie's face. She felt like an intruder horning in on two lovers' private moment.

"Cut it out, you guys," Cassie said when Nick buried his face in his wife's neck. "This isn't a nice thing to do to a single woman with no prospects." She immediately thought about Brendan and fought back a rush of excitement and apprehension about seeing him again.

Nick looked at her with surprise. "Hey, Cassie, I happen to know more than a few guys—"

The elevator pinged and the doors slid open, saving Cassie from Nick Kempner's offer to rescue her from the cesspool of self-imposed celibacy by finding her "a man." They traveled down the hall and pushed through the double doors and into the area immediately outside the Neonatal Intensive Care Unit. In the nearby waiting room they found Dr.

Jared Granger standing over his wife, Brooke, who was seated in a chair holding a bundle of soft blue blanket. Next to Jared stood Jeanie and Howard Lewis, proud-grandparent smiles plastered on their faces.

Cassie released a breath of relief when she noted that Brendan wasn't anywhere around. That fact also brought about disappointment. Just as well, she supposed.

Michelle hovered over the baby, cooing like a mourning dove. Cassie made her way to Brooke who pulled back the blanket, revealing the tiny baby boy with a small cap of downy blond hair and one hand curled against his cheek, his eyes struggling to focus against the harsh fluorescent light.

Warmth flooded Cassie's chest, and longing gripped her heart. "He's beautiful, Brooke. I know you're thrilled to finally be taking him home."

Brooke looked from her son to Cassie, her eyes misty. "Two months is a long time to wait. But it was worth it." She gazed at her husband with adoration. "We did good, didn't we, Daddy?"

"No, we did great." Jared leaned down and brushed a tender kiss across Brooke's cheek, then did the same to his son.

A few people might overdose on all the love radiating from this family, but not Cassie. She craved being a part of something so special. Thoughts of the mother she had never known filtered into her consciousness as she watched the group gather round to discuss who little Matthew Granger favored. The general consensus was Howard Lewis, due to the baby's sparse hair and chubby cheeks.

Cassie shared in the laughter while wondering

what her own mother had been thinking when she'd left three days after Cassie's birth. Had she realized that her careless disregard had left her then-husband a bitter man who'd never been able to make an emotional commitment to his only child? And in turn, Cassie had tried to find love in all the wrong places, a mistake she still paid for even after years of trying to right that wrong by being a success in her career, a faithful daughter. Futile attempts to earn her father's respect, even if she couldn't earn his love. She never had, and she'd finally come to realize that she never would.

She had also come to terms with the fact that she'd never know her mother after learning through relatives that the woman who'd borne her, then deserted her, had died two years ago.

At least the Granger baby would never have to experience such heartache, never lack in the love department.

"You ready to go, Brooke?" Jared asked, drawing Cassie out of her melancholy remembrance.

"Sure, but I want to thank Dr. O'Connor first."

"No thanks needed. Just send me a picture now and then to add to my collection."

Cassie looked from the baby to Brendan, and her heart took a plunge. She routinely came in contact with him on a daily basis, but today was different. He looked the same, still gorgeous with that even-tempered aura everyone had come to respect and admire. His staff adored him and so did his patients' parents. Though the stress level in the NICU was off the scale, morale was high on that unit, all because of Dr. Brendan O'Connor's grace under fire.

Brendan shook Nick and Jared's hand then his

gaze met Cassie's. He gave her a slight smile and a guarded look that told her he was remembering last night, too. Or maybe she was reading too much into it.

After handing Jared a vinyl case, Brendan said, "Here's the apnea monitor. Any questions?"

"Millie gave us instructions," Jared said. "We'll let you know if anything comes up."

Jeanie Lewis stepped forward, wringing her hands. "Doctor, do you think he's well enough to go home? Since his lungs—"

"He's fine, Mrs. Lewis." Brendan sent her a reassuring smile, revealing his little-boy dimple. "The monitor's a precautionary measure. It's only for a little while to make sure everything's okay. Try not to worry."

Howard Lewis laughed, taking Cassie by surprise. The man rarely got a word in edgewise with his wife's penchant for chatter. "That's like telling a politician not to make promises."

They all laughed then, except for Jeanie Lewis. But the laughter died when a nurse rushed through the NICU doors. "Dr. O'Connor. The Neely baby's crashing."

Brendan spun around and said, "Good luck," then disappeared through the unit entrance.

A heavy silence settled over the group until Jared said, "Let's get out of here."

Cassie followed the party down to the lobby and said her goodbyes, then returned to her first-floor office. She made a few necessary phone calls, all the while worrying about the Neely's critically ill baby, and Brendan.

An hour later she received the news that Brendan

had pulled the baby through the latest crisis and that the Neelys were waiting on five, in dire need of some consolation.

Cassie returned to the fifth floor and spoke with the frazzled parents, doing her very best to assure them that their daughter was receiving excellent care under Dr. O'Connor's expert guidance. She encouraged them to go to the cafeteria for some coffee; they would be paged if anything changed. When they insisted on staying nearby, Cassie set out to find Brendan.

She donned a paper gown and entered the NICU. Once inside, she conducted a visual search and encountered the usual flurry of activity among the staff, several she acknowledged with a brief greeting. Sounds of periodic alarms and the hiss of ventilators rang in her ears. In the most critical area, rows of transparent incubators held babies of all sizes and conditions, some so small they were barely visible among all the lines and tubes. A few parents sat near the tiny beds, touching with care in an attempt to bond with their babies, infants who could not be held because of the detriment to their fragile conditions.

Time suspended in this place of heartache and hope. Cassie had seen it all before, the sadness, the joy, the precious battle for life from the smallest of warriors. She had dealt with disheartened parents and provided bereavement counseling when necessary, all facets of her job. Yet she didn't know if she could deal with the stress of caring for sick babies on a daily basis. How did Brendan do it, day in and day out?

When she didn't immediately see Brendan, Cassie

approached one of the nurses crouched in front of a supply cabinet. "Excuse me, Millie."

The woman looked back, and recognition dawned in her expression. She smiled. "Hi, Cassie. What can I do for you?"

"I just finished speaking with the Neelys. How's their little girl doing?"

Millie glanced at a nearby crib where another nurse and respiratory therapist stood close by monitoring the baby girl. "Okay, for now. Dr. O'Connor worked like the devil to bring her around. That guy is amazing."

Cassie couldn't agree more. "Do you know where he is?"

"He left a while ago after talking to the parents." She nodded toward a man at the end of the aisle. "Dr. Segovia's relieving him."

"Did Dr. O'Connor say where he was going?"

Millie shrugged. "Home, I guess. He wanted to stick around but Segovia told him to get out of here."

Cassie's concern increased ten-fold. "Is he okay?"

Millie's brows drew down beneath the blue cap covering her salt-and-pepper hair. "I probably shouldn't mention this, but he really did need to go. Normally he's pretty calm under pressure, but today he was a wreck, barking orders at everyone. He's got the whole department in an uproar. In the year that he's been here, I've never seen him like that before."

"For some reason he's taking this one hard."

"Maybe the whole atmosphere is finally getting

to him. This place can be a hotbed for burnout, I tell you."

Cassie intended to find out exactly what was going on with Brendan and what she could do to help. "I'll see you around, Millie. If anything happens with the Neely baby, have someone call me at home or on my cell phone. I'll come back in."

"Sure thing, Cassie."

Bent on a mission, Cassie hurried back to her office and gathered a few files she could work on at home. She picked up the phone and dialed Brendan's number. No answer. Although she'd never been to his apartment, he'd told her that he lived not more than ten minutes away. Maybe he stopped somewhere to have a drink or dinner. She hated to think about him doing either alone.

After she pounded out his cell phone number, his voice mail kicked in. Cassie opted not to leave a message. She would go home and try again. And again and again until she reached him, even if it took all night.

He kicked the dumpster twice in an attempt to expend some of his anger. Not finding any relief, Brendan turned the anger on his car, pounding his fist into the door. The shooting pain in his knuckles did nothing to alleviate his frustration, his fury.

He braced his palms on the top of the sedan and lowered his head, relieved that no one was in the outdoor parking lot to play witness to his stupidity.

The emotions were no strangers. They came calling the same time each year. Today had been worse than before, compounded by his efforts to save an infant barely hanging on to a slender thread of life, knowing that it might be only a matter of time before the baby lost her battle.

Even though he fought against his own well-guarded memories, they came rushing back on a surge of bitter recollections, his experience as fresh in his mind as if it had happened yesterday.

Thirteen years ago he had lost his baby son.

That loss had led him to his career, driven by a powerful need to never let anyone suffer the same anguish of watching their child die, if he could help it. But he wasn't God, and although there had been many victories, the failures still ate at his soul like potent acid.

"Brendan?" Cassie's cotton-soft voice floated in on the breeze from behind him.

He was suddenly caught between wanting to tell her to go away and leave him to his misery, and an overwhelming need for her to stay. He could use her strength right now but he had no right to ask. Not after last night.

Slowly he turned to face her, the setting sun burnishing her blond hair, turning it to a rich gold. She looked beautiful in that moment, and worried.

Her eyes widened as she zeroed in on his hand. "You're bleeding!"

He hadn't even noticed the trickle of blood trailing down his arm. "I'm okay. It's only a scrape."

Her expression was grim. "No, you're not okay. What are you still doing here? Millie told me you'd gone home."

He leaned back against the car and swiped his arm against his thigh, leaving a streak of blood on his scrub pants. "I locked my damned keys in the car."

She walked over to him and gently clasped his

hand in hers to examine his wound. "And you decided to beat the door down?"

"Something like that."

"Leave the car here and come home with me. I can clean this up for you."

He yanked his hand from her grasp and immediately regretted the action when he noted the hurt in her eyes. "I'll take care of it. I'll call security and get them to unlock the door."

"I don't care about your car. I do care about you. You look like you've lost your best friend."

No, he hadn't, at least not yet. She was standing right in front of him. "It's been a really sorry day, Cassie."

"I know it has," she said in that quiet counselor's voice he'd heard her use on other people, and even at times on him. "That's why you need to come to my place. I'll fix you some dinner and we can watch one of those trauma shows."

"Nothing like taking your work home with you."

She shrugged and smiled. "We can find some cable channel and watch dirty movies. Or cartoons. Doesn't matter to me."

Watching dirty movies wasn't something Brendan cared to do with Cassie. Not with the way he was feeling—frustrated and looking for a way to vent that frustration. Sex wasn't an option, especially not with Cassie. Not that he wouldn't like to make love to her, long and hard and all night. He wouldn't risk it. He'd already taken one too many chances, made one too many mistakes. Enough to last a lifetime.

But he didn't really want to be alone, either. Cassie had a way about her, the means to make him forget. Right now he needed to forget, if only for a while. "Okay, I'll have dinner with you. *After* I call security and have them unlock my car. Otherwise, you'll have to bring me back."

"Suit yourself." She rummaged through her purse and withdrew a business card, then scrawled something on the back. After she was done, she handed it to him. "Here's my address. It's easy to find. Just look for the smallest house."

He studied the card. "You live in a house?"

"Yes, why?"

He met her gaze once again. "I don't know. I figured you for the swinging-single-apartment type."

"Well, you figured wrong."

"Do you have a roommate?"

"No, it's just little old me."

That both relieved and worried Brendan. An empty house and Cassie could be a lethal combination, especially with the way he was feeling. Not if he kept his wits about him, exactly what he intended to do. What he *had* to do.

"I'll see you in a while then," she said as she turned away. After taking a few steps, she faced him again. "Oh, I do have a cat, in case you're allergic."

"No, I'm not allergic. But I hate cats."

She grinned. "Don't worry. He hates everyone but me."

Three

The cat loved Brendan. No great surprise to Cassie. Everyone loved Brendan, so why wouldn't a crazed cat?

Still, she'd never seen Mister snuggle up to a man. Of course, the men in Cassie's life had been very few and very far between, at least since high school. Other than a rare visit from her dad, no man had sat on her couch since that day the kitty had shown up on her doorstep, begging for handouts. And Mister definitely did not care for her father. Maybe the animal sensed that Cassie's dad didn't really care for Cassie. Smart cat.

Cassie stood at the kitchen entrance to the living room and watched Mister rub against Brendan as if he were a treat. She couldn't blame him. She actually wanted to join him. Rubbing against Brendan would be the highlight of her evening. That certainly would make her purr. But she wouldn't. She'd simply fantasize about it later, after he left. Safer that way.

Brendan just sat there, eyeing the overly friendly feline with mild disgust. At least the doctor looked more relaxed now than he had at dinner. He'd said very little during the meal of pasta and salad, something Cassie had whipped up with a jar of sauce and the greens she'd had on hand. Not exactly her idea of a romantic meal. Of course, her offer had nothing to do with romance. She was only trying to provide Brendan with some company and comfort.

On that thought, Cassie tossed the dishtowel onto the cabinet and strolled into the small living room. She took a seat on the couch opposite Brendan and Mister.

Brendan awkwardly patted the enamored cat's head with his bandaged hand. "Does this walking hairball have a name?"

"Mister Ree."

"Mystery?"

"No. Two words, Mister *R-e-e*."

"Weird name."

"Not really. His background is a mystery. I have no idea where he came from. He just showed up one day two years ago, and he's been here ever since."

"Do you always pick up strays?"

"Only cats. And every now and then a man who's locked his keys in the car."

Brendan frowned. "So you bring men home often?"

"I'm kidding. If you recall, we've already had this conversation about my love life, or lack thereof."

Cassie leaned over and pulled Mister out of Brendan's lap with some difficulty when the cat decided to hang on. The doctor looked more than relieved.

"Time to go outside." She stood and opened the door, and Mister scurried out.

"He's sure in a hurry," Brendan said. "Must be some hot kitty waiting for him."

Cassie reclaimed her place on the end of the sofa. "He's neutered."

Brendan grinned. "Do you do that to all your guests?"

She leaned her head back and laughed, then brought her gaze back to his sparkling green eyes. "You betcha. Helps to keep the population of unwanted offspring down."

Brendan's features switched from relaxed to serious as easily as one would click off a lamp. The glow of amusement had left his eyes, as well. "Probably not a bad idea at that."

Scooting around on the sofa to face him, Cassie crossed her legs in front of her, determined to wipe the frustration away from his face. "I spoke to the Neelys this afternoon. They're so grateful to you for bringing their baby back around."

His mouth formed an unforgiving line to match his grave expression. "Back around to what? A child that might be blind? Chronic pulmonary problems because of a respirator?"

She hated the sadness in his tone, in his eyes. "Would you like to know what Mrs. Neely said to me today?" When he didn't respond, she continued. "She told me that she's had three previous miscarriages. This pregnancy was the closest she's carried to full term. She also told me that no matter what happens to her little girl, as long as she can bring her home, she'll deal with any lingering problems when the time comes.''

Brendan sighed. "Knowing what could happen doesn't make dealing with it any easier.''

"I realize that, and so does she." Cassie drew in a breath and forced back the threatening tears over Mrs. Neely's parting words. "She also told me, 'God's given me a baby who needs me as much as I need her.'''

Brendan leaned forward, rested his elbows on his knees and lowered his head into the cradle of his hands. The silence was excruciating while Cassie sat helpless, waiting for him to speak, wondering what she could do to make him feel better.

When he failed to raise his head, she slipped behind him on her knees and rested her hands on his broad shoulders to try and knead the tension away. "I hate seeing you this way, Brendan. Talk to me.''

"I couldn't help him..." His words trailed off on a lingering sigh.

"Him? You mean her, don't you? The Neely baby?''

"No, I mean..." He expelled another broken breath then straightened as if trying to recover. "It was years ago, and it doesn't matter. It's over.''

No, it wasn't over, at least not for him, whatever "it" was. She suspected he was thinking back to another baby, probably one he didn't save. Most likely something he deemed a failure, a circumstance that had stuck with him even after a long passage of time.

Cassie had been trained to handle such instances with patients, most of them strangers, but Brendan wasn't a stranger. Still, she wouldn't push him for more information than he was capable of giving. She hoped that by allowing him space and time, he would eventually talk to her. At the moment she only wanted to comfort him, get him past this particular crisis.

Cassie tightened her hold on him. "Tell me what you need, Brendan. Tell me what I can do to help."

Looking back with a soulful gaze, he twined his fingers with hers. "I need you, Cassie. Only you."

She moved into his lap then and held him, her heart breaking for the strong yet troubled doctor. Turning her face up, she accepted his sudden kiss. Not the same kiss from the night before. This one was full of frustration, fueled by Brendan's despair. His hold on her tightened, as if he feared she might pull away. She had no desire to do that.

But could she risk it all by letting the intimacy continue? What would tomorrow bring if she did? An end to their relationship, or the beginning of something more, something deeper? If she took the plunge, the ultimate chance, would she find herself landing in love? Or was it already too late?

Taking Cassie by surprise, Brendan moved her aside and rose from the sofa. He held out his hand to her. "Come with me."

"Where are we going?"

"To your bedroom."

Shock momentarily stole her voice. "Brendan, I'm not sure that's—"

"Just for a while, Cassie. I need to hold you. I'm beat."

Cassie stood, questions racing around in her head, yet she took his hand and led him in silence to the

darkened bedroom. Once there, he turned her into
his arms and kissed her again, this time more gently.
But she felt his despair as keenly as if it were her
own.

Backing to the bed, he pulled her down to join
him. They stretched out and faced each other, bodies
and emotions intertwined, surrounded by comfortable darkness and welcome silence. She soon became lost in more of Brendan's intoxicating kisses.

Deep down Cassie knew she should stop this before it went any further. Before she made the same
mistake again, giving all of herself to Brendan
knowing it could ruin the friendship, knowing he
probably couldn't give her more. Knowing that she
would become even more emotionally drawn in to
his world, probably to her own detriment.

Thankfully, he seemed content to only hold her
close, but he continued to kiss her. Then he set his
hands in motion over her back, trailed touches over
the dip of her spine, caressed her bottom for a time,
curled his fingertips between her thighs. His touch
grew more insistent, carried her away from reality,
from past lapses in judgment that seemed intent on
repeating themselves. But this was Brendan touching her, Brendan holding her, something she had
only imagined in her most secret fantasies.

From the sound of Brendan's rapid breathing, his
insistent kisses, she sensed he was nearing the edge,
barely clinging to a fragile thread of restraint. So
was she, and then suddenly the thread broke. They
undressed with abandon, his scrubs and briefs, her
sweatshirt, pants and underwear, until nothing came
between them except warm flesh contacting warm
flesh.

With a rough groan, Brendan rose above her, nudged her legs apart with a hair-roughened thigh and buried himself inside her. At first her body reacted with a spark of discomfort from the sudden sensual invasion. But as he held her close and whispered her name, she was struck with a sense of pleasure, of wonder, like nothing she had ever known before.

His thrusts grew almost desperate, all consuming. "I need you, Cassie," he said, his words shot through with an agony that Cassie felt in the deepest reaches of her soul.

"I'm here, Brendan," she told him over and over, trying desperately to absorb some of his pain.

He trailed kisses across her neck and settled his lips on her breast. Cassie surrendered to the blissful moment, immersed herself in the rhythm, welcomed the intimacy and Brendan's strength. She held fast to him, not daring to examine the feelings bubbling up inside her—a deep-seated longing—and love. A love that she had hidden from him, from herself for several months, until now.

Cassie was so close to the edge, wanting the sensations to go on forever, but they ended much too soon. With one last thrust and a moan, Brendan collapsed against her.

Neither of them moved as several seconds counted down in time with the ticking bedside clock, in sync with Cassie's galloping pulse. Her heart raced frantically when she suddenly realized what they had done.

She hadn't looked beyond the moment, beyond providing comfort. Nor had she considered the consequences. What should she do now? What would Brendan do?

Cassie knew the moment awareness hit Brendan. She sensed it in the tightening of his frame, the long sigh from his lips that now rested against her neck, and the single word, "Damn," that came out in a harsh whisper.

Brendan slipped from her body, sat up and streaked both hands through his hair. "What in the hell have I done?"

Cassie draped her legs over the edge of the bed, scooted beside him and laid a palm on his shoulder. "It wasn't only you, Brendan."

He shrugged off her hand. "But I know better."

She flipped on the bedside lamp and sighed. "Like I don't? We're both responsible for what happened."

He focused on the watercolor painting hanging on the wall across the room, his hands fisted on his bare thighs. "Are you on the Pill?"

"I was. Low dose to regulate my periods. But I haven't been taking them for three months."

"That's what I was afraid of." He sounded afraid.

"Pregnancy's not our only concern."

He still wouldn't look at her. "You don't have to worry about that. I'm safe."

"So am I." She didn't feel at all safe, not from an emotional standpoint. The intangible wall Brendan had raised concerned her almost as much as the threat of pregnancy. They should be holding each other in the aftermath, not debating the possible outcome. Maybe at some other time, some other place, that might actually happen. But not now.

She had intended to give him comfort, not cause

him more pain. But that's exactly what she had done. "Look, Brendan, odds are nothing will come of this."

He yanked on his scrubs then pushed off the bed to pace. "What if we defy the odds and you end up pregnant?"

"I'll deal with it."

Halting before her, he said, "*We'll* deal with it. You have to swear to me that you'll tell me if you are."

"Of course I'll tell you. But that's something we shouldn't worry about now. No need to borrow trouble."

"I am worried. Damned worried."

So was she, about many things, the least of which was the possible detriment to their relationship. How could a few moments of bliss that had felt so right, at least to Cassie, turn out to be so wrong? "Let's take it one day at a time, okay?"

His gaze traveled slowly over her flushed body, his eyes full of concern. "Did I hurt you? I was pretty rough."

Suddenly self-conscious over his steady perusal, Cassie grabbed the comforter to cover herself. "Of course you didn't hurt me."

"But I didn't do that much for you, either."

"I'm fine, Brendan. Really."

He took a seat next to her and clasped her hand between his large palms. "I'm an idiot, Cassie. I wouldn't blame you if you hated me now."

She rested her head on his shoulder. "I could never hate you, no matter what."

"But you didn't even—"

"It doesn't matter."

"Dammit, it does matter. You deserve better."

Normally she would agree. She preferred slow seduction, a little romance, long kisses, lots of foreplay, something she'd never really had before. But this hadn't been a normal circumstance. Brendan didn't realize that making love with him had meant a great deal to her, a union that had little to do with the physical and all to do with the emotional. He would never understand that. Most men wouldn't.

"I'm not going to break in two over this, Brendan."

"No big deal, right?" he asked with a good deal of sarcasm.

She certainly couldn't admit to that because it wasn't at all true. "More like just one of those things."

He took her into his arms and stroked her hair with tenderness. The Brendan she knew—and loved—was back, at least for the moment. "I can't stand the thought of losing our friendship over this."

Friendship. She couldn't stand the thought of losing him, even if she had to pretend that she considered him only a friend. After tonight she considered him to be much, much more.

"We're going to be okay, Brendan," she assured him. "Everything's going to be okay."

It was anything but okay.

Cassie sat at her desk, staring at the lab results with Brendan's insistent words running through her mind.

Swear to me that you'll tell me if you're pregnant.

The question had hung between them for the past two months, even though neither of them had voiced it. They had gone about the business of trying to act normal, at work and during their tennis games. Cassie had believed that maybe they would get past what had happened that night. Brendan hadn't kissed her again, much less touched her, no matter how much she had ached for his kiss and touch. Back to normal, or so it appeared on the surface. Cassie would never feel normal around him again.

And now, knowing she was carrying his baby caused a sharp fear to impale her heart. What would he do when she told him? Would he walk away like her mother had? Shut her off like her father? Would he retreat further into himself?

Soon she would know. Fifteen minutes ago she'd summoned him to her office. And now she waited with her heart in her throat, perspiring palms and a determination to keep herself together while facing Brendan. She could fall apart later.

Cassie heard the doctor's deep voice greeting the receptionist outside her door. She gripped the edge of her seat and drew in a cleansing breath.

Still she jumped when the door opened and Brendan stepped inside. At least he was smiling. She wondered how long that would last once she lowered the boom.

"What's up?" he asked as he took the seat across from her.

"You look happy. What's up with you?"

His grin expanded. "Monica Neely turned the corner this morning. Looks like she's out of the woods."

"That's great, Brendan." Even though she'd tried to sound pleased, her words came out stiff, lacking in enthusiasm.

Brendan studied her a long moment. "What's wrong?"

"I'm pregnant."

His smile faltered, replaced by a stunned look, as if someone had slapped him. In a way she had with her sudden outburst.

"Are you sure?" he asked.

She slid the lab slip in front of him. "As sure as I can be. I did an over-the-counter test first, then confirmed that this morning in the lab."

"But it's been two months, Cassie. Why did you wait so long?"

She shrugged. "I've never been very regular. I guess I thought... I don't know what I thought. Maybe I've been in denial."

Brendan bolted from his chair and walked to the window, lifting the blinds to reveal the overcast skies. "I should've known this would happen."

The anger in his tone sliced her heart as sharply as a razor. "I'm sorry, Brendan." It was all she could think to say at the moment.

"No, I'm the one who should be sorry. I screwed up."

Cassie could no longer contain the rush of hot tears. She had vowed not to cry. She needed to be strong and not let him see how she was crumbling inside. But she was crumbling, inside and out.

He turned to her and started to speak, then his mouth dropped shut. Walking to the desk, he held out his hand to her. "Come here."

She stood and went easily into his strong arms, her tears dampening the front of his lab coat. He held her tightly and rubbed her back until she finally regained some composure.

Staring up at him, she posed the question foremost in her mind. "What do you want to do?"

"I wish the hell I knew."

Not the answer she had longed for. Not by a long shot.

Cassie stepped out of his arms and reclaimed her chair, fearing her limbs might not hold her much longer. "We have time to think about it. I'm only a couple of months along."

He looked alarmed. "You're not considering terminating the pregnancy, are you?"

"No! I want this baby, Brendan." And she did, with all her heart.

He looked as though he didn't believe her. "What about your work? You told me that you didn't plan on having any children for a long time."

She swiped away a few rogue tears. "That was before." Before she had lost a good deal of her heart to him. Before she was having *his* child. "I'll do whatever I have to do to make it work out."

"Am I included in your plans?"

"That's entirely up to you."

He propped his hands on the desk and leaned into them. "I need time to think, Cassie. Right now I can't do that. I've got to get back to work."

In a way she regretted not waiting until the end of the day to deliver the news. But, considering the fact she'd used the local laboratory for the test, someone could possibly have spilled the information if she'd chosen to wait. The hospital grapevine traveled at the speed of light despite most employees' discretion. She hadn't been willing to risk Brendan hearing it from someone else.

"Can you meet me after work?" she asked.

"Yeah. I'll call you before I leave the unit."

She stood and joined him at the door. "Whatever you decide, Brendan, I'll honor it. If you want to bow out, you won't have to worry that I'll make your life miserable."

Uncertainty passed over his expression. "Thing is, Cassie, it would probably be the other way around."

Brendan spent the rest of the day running on autopilot, trying not to think about Cassie's news. Trying to forget her tears, her worry. He hadn't been successful. Luckily the NICU had been relatively quiet. No major catastrophes, not even a new admission.

But as his shift ended, serious concerns came home to roost. He headed into the hospital courtyard immediately outside the NICU waiting room and took a seat on a lone concrete bench. He needed to think before facing Cassie again.

The place was deserted, probably because a steady mist fell from the dismal skies. The atmosphere suited his dark mood. For a moment he considered trying to get in touch with his mom and dad. They had been supportive during a time when he'd needed them most. He nixed that idea. They were traveling abroad, and he didn't want to ruin their well-deserved time together. Although his parents wouldn't judge him, he couldn't stomach the thought of letting them down once again. He couldn't stand the thought of letting Cassie down, either.

Thoughts of that day thirteen years ago came calling once again, no matter how hard he tried to keep them at bay. His son had lived for a few hours, born too small, too weak to survive.

At first he'd laid the blame on Jill for not seeking prenatal care. Now he'd come to realize that he had been to blame, too. Although he hadn't known about Jill's pregnancy, oftentimes he'd wondered how he would have handled the situation if he had known. He hadn't really given Jill any reason to let him know. He'd broken off the relationship and all communication after one night when she'd tried to convince him that she couldn't live without him—the night they had made a child because of his carelessness.

Back then he had walked away. He'd been focused only on his goal of becoming a doctor, a nineteen-year-old college kid with no real means of support for a wife and child. Not exactly the case at the present, although his time was still at a premium and his funds limited, since he had so little tenure at the hospital and a few college loans that still needed to be paid. But he made enough to provide for a family if he had to, even if it meant working extra shifts.

He raised his face to the sky and welcomed the cold, chastising himself for making the same mistake again. Only this time he wasn't a kid; he was an adult. And Cassie was nothing like Jill. She had been trying to provide him with comfort, not to tie him down. She needed him to be there for her, for their child.

Regardless, the prospect of having another baby settled like a boulder in Brendan's gut. Could he be a good father? Would he survive if something happened to this child? Could he ever get beyond his fears and give her what she needed?

He lived with huge risks every day when dealing with his patients. That was different. He did what he had to do because he couldn't do anything else. He didn't want to do anything else. But the baby Cassie now carried was *his* child.

The answer to his dilemma became all too clear. He could make up for past mistakes by doing the right thing. He could atone somewhat for his failures by trying hard not to fail again. He had no choice but to face his responsibility head-on this time, and hope against hope he could do right by Cassie.

Determination sent him forward in a rush. He opted not to wait for the elevator and took the stairs to the first floor instead. By the time he reached Cassie's office, his heart pummeled his chest. His breathing came hard and heavy, both from physical exertion and fear over Cassie's reaction to what he was about to propose.

He sent a cursory wave at the gaping receptionist and pushed into Cassie's office. When he shut the door behind him, Cassie glanced up, surprise in her expression. "I thought you were going to call."

"I needed to do this in person."

Her face fell as if it had the weight of the world attached. "Okay. So do it."

He took her hands and pulled her up. Calling up his courage, he surveyed the beautiful face of his best friend—and the mother of his unborn child.

"Marry me, Cassie."

Four

Cassie's heart lodged in her throat, blocking any kind of verbal response to Brendan's out-of-the-blue proposal.

This wasn't at all what she had expected when he'd rushed into her office. She had primed herself for a graceful goodbye. Maybe not a "So long, see you around"—she really didn't believe Brendan would leave her high and dry, alone and pregnant—but she certainly hadn't anticipated him asking her to marry him.

He tipped up her chin to meet his serious gaze. "Well?"

Her voice finally came back to her, along with the realization he was waiting for an answer she wasn't quite ready to give. She still had questions. Many, many questions. "Why would you want to marry me, other than the fact that I'm pregnant?"

He paused for a moment, his hands still tightly gripping hers. "Because it's the right thing to do for our baby."

She pulled away from his physical hold, but he still held her emotionally imprisoned. "What about us?"

He looked away for a brief moment before bringing his attention back to her. "I'm not saying I have all the answers, Cassie. I'm saying this is a start."

"A start to what? A union of obligation for the sake of a child?"

"Another step in our relationship."

"A huge step."

"I don't deny that, but I think we have to take it." He braced both hands on her shoulders. "I care a lot about you, Cassie. I want to be there for you through this whole process."

"And after that?"

"We'll take it as it comes. One day at a time."

Hadn't *she* told him that? Right after she'd made love with him, and in turn, made a baby. "I need some time, Brendan. I have to know that if we decide to go through with this, we're going to be in it for the long haul. I couldn't take it if you decided to leave once the baby's born."

He looked hurt, confused. "Why do you think I'd do that?"

"Because you would have no reason to stay."

Now he looked angry. "You're my best friend. I can't think of anyone else I'd rather be around."

Cassie thought he might as well have said, *You're a great gal, Cassie. Lots of fun on the courts. Nice to have a beer with now and then.* "It will be different between us, Brendan. No one really knows everything about someone unless they live with them.''

''Exactly. That's why we need to get married.''

Flawed logic, as far as Cassie was concerned. ''Do we really need a license? Maybe we should just live together for a while. See how it works out.''

''No way. We have reputations to uphold here at the hospital.''

Now she was getting to the crux of the matter. Brendan valued his blessed reputation in the medical community. Shacking up with someone, having a baby out of wedlock, even in modern times, might ruin that for him. ''Well, my goodness, we wouldn't want to sully your good name, would we?''

''Cassie, you're not being fair.''

He was right. This wasn't fair. The one thing she wanted to hear him say, needed to hear him say, hadn't come. But what could she expect? Yes, he did care about her, and they were good friends, but was that enough? Would it ever be enough for her if she never had Brendan's love?

She needed more time to consider what he offered—a marriage and two parents for her baby. A marriage that held no promise of forever. Her decision would be based on what was best for her child. After all, she hadn't been afforded that opportunity where her own parents were concerned.

''Okay, Brendan,'' she said with resignation. ''I'll think about it.''

He looked hopeful. ''Great. I want to take you to dinner tonight. We can talk more then.''

She laid a hand on her chest. ''Why, Dr. O'Connor, do you mean a real date?''

He smiled. ''Come to think of it, that's exactly

what I mean. We can go to that bistro on Carnes Street.''

A romantic place, Cassie thought. Intimate, expensive. A good place to talk about getting married. She couldn't escape the tiny thrill running through her even though she was determined to stay grounded in reality.

Then Cassie remembered another obligation. A monthly obligation that she dreaded, but something she couldn't avoid. ''It will have to be later, and I'll need to meet you there. I have something I have to do first.''

''Take the first train out of town?'' He sounded as if he was teasing, but he looked much too serious.

''I'm not going to run away, if that's what you're worried about.''

She had run away from her problems before, escaped the realities of life, almost to her own detriment. She refused to do that again. Somehow she would find a way to do the right thing for her child without regard to what she desired—Dr. Brendan O'Connor's love.

The room was dusty and dim, illuminated only by the blue glow from a television screen. The lingering scent of stale cigarette smoke and the vibrations of underlying hostility made Cassie want to turn around and never look back. But she wouldn't do that. She had always come back, returned to face the sins of the past and her father's judgment.

She approached the lounger where her father reclined, dozing, a beer on the table next to him.

Coy Allen loved his beer—one of the few things he loved.

"Dad?" Her voice sounded shaky, unsure.

His eyes drifted open and he leveled an unfocused gaze on her. "Must be Thursday," he grumbled.

"Yeah, it's Thursday." She perched on the edge of the sofa and folded her hands in her lap. "Did you go to the doctor?"

He ran a hand over his close-cropped hair. "He saw me."

"What did he say?"

"Same old thing. Quit smoking. Lose weight."

None of which he had done, Cassie thought as her gaze wandered to the ashtray overflowing with butts. "Probably good advice considering your heart problem."

Without responding, he picked up his beer and took a swig, his gaze leveled on the TV. As usual, Cassie was all but invisible to him. She didn't know why she still tried to reach him, maybe out of obligation because he was her father. Maybe because he was the only family she had.

There had been times in the distant past when he'd let down his guard, but they were few and far between. Still, Cassie clung to the hope that one day he would stop blaming her for his wife's departure and that they could mend their relationship, especially now that she was going to have a baby.

On that thought, she shored up all her courage to deliver the news. "I have something to tell you, Dad."

His response was little more than a grunt.

Cassie placed a protective hand over her belly, as if she could shield her unborn child from her father's bitterness. "You're going to be a grandfather."

His gaze snapped from the screen to her, but she

didn't see happiness. Nothing new there. "Who got you pregnant?"

"Actually, a man I've been seeing for a while now. A good man. A successful doctor." She sounded like the desperate little girl again.

See, Daddy? I painted you a picture. See, Daddy? I made all As on my report card. Guess what, Dad? I received my master's degree.

It had never been enough.

With his attention back on the football game, he said, "Doesn't surprise me none you're pregnant. I figured it would've happened before now."

Cassie flinched at his condescension. She refused to become that lonely, frightened teenager again, the one who had made mistakes while searching for validation in the arms of a no-account boy. Attention that she'd never received from her own flesh and blood.

"He's asked me to marry him," she added, her tone defiant, as if Coy Allen really cared. He didn't care about anything but being left alone with his miserable existence.

He shrugged and stretched, then propped his hands on his undershirt-covered belly. "So? Don't mean he's going to stick around after you have the kid."

In that moment Cassie wanted desperately to hate him. But as always, she wouldn't allow that emotion. His sadness, his bitterness over something that had happened years before, had made him a pitiful shell of a man. And since his retirement, he had only gotten worse. But he had no one but her. No one to take care of him if his health deteriorated.

Cassie tolerated his apathy because if she left him

alone, perhaps to die, she would never be able to live with herself. She supposed he was already dead in a way, at least inside, thanks to Cassie's mother.

Silence stretched between them for a few moments before he asked, "You going to marry him?"

A very good question. Was she going to marry Brendan? Was her father right, Brendan would leave after the baby was born?

But Brendan wasn't her mother, and she certainly wasn't her father. For her baby's sake, she would take the chance that she and Brendan could make it work. Prove to her father that she wasn't the reckless girl she'd once been. Prove to him that not everyone walked out on their responsibilities, their life. Their child.

Cassie stood clutching her purse and feeling a strong sense of pity for the man before her who had left her a long time ago, at least emotionally. Her father might not be happy, but she would do everything she could to make sure her child would be happy. And most of all loved, even if Cassie wasn't.

"As a matter of fact, Dad, yes, I am going to marry him."

Brendan sat at the table for two with sweaty palms and a hot face. At least he hadn't come down with cold feet. Yet.

Thankfully only a few people dined in the restaurant tonight, giving him and Cassie some privacy. If she ever got there. He checked his watch once more. Half past eight. She was already forty-five minutes late.

Maybe she had reconsidered. Maybe she'd caught that train or plane or bus out of town. He couldn't blame her if she decided to leave him behind after what he had done to her. Done to them both.

The sound of the familiar voice coming from the maître d's podium near the door drew Brendan's attention. He glanced up to see Cassie walking toward him, looking as elegant as the surroundings.

He'd never seen her dressed like this before—in black satin and high heels. The dress, although long-sleeved, was cut low in front, accentuating her round breasts and outlining every curve to perfection. Her golden hair glimmered underneath the lights along with her dark eyes complemented by makeup that she rarely wore.

Brendan had always liked the way Cassie looked in tennis attire, fresh-faced and natural. But he could more than appreciate this side of her. Tonight she exuded sensuality. Sex. Tonight she could bring a man to his knees in ten seconds, not ten minutes. Luckily he was still seated.

She moved with grace and confidence. But when she drew closer, he noticed the wariness in her dark eyes.

Standing, he pulled back her chair. "Hi."

"Hi. Sorry I'm late."

She slipped into the chair, and he pushed it forward before reclaiming his own seat.

"Did you get everything taken care of?" he asked.

She immediately picked up the menu, avoiding his gaze. "Yes. As well as I could."

Curiosity got the best of Brendan. So did his concern for her. "If you don't mind telling me, where did you go?"

She glanced up from the menu for a brief moment

before studying it once again. "I had to see my father."

"Yeah? You've never mentioned him before. I didn't know he was in town."

She set the menu in front of her and rested her folded hands on it. "Oh, yeah, he's here." Her tone was less than thrilled over that fact.

"Problems?" Brendan asked.

"No more than usual. He's a mess healthwise. Smokes two packs a day, drinks beer, eats junk. He doesn't leave his lounge chair unless he needs to go to the store to restock."

Something else in her demeanor urged Brendan to question her more. "Do you guys get along otherwise?"

She sent him a cynical smile. "Oh, sure. As long as I don't bother him more than once a month. He's never cared to be in my presence for very long."

"What about your mom?"

Cassie gave a one-shoulder shrug. "She hightailed it out of town when I was three days old. I haven't seen her since, and I found out she died two years ago."

Brendan hated the pain in her voice. Hated the fact that, unlike him, she'd had the misfortune to be born to uncaring parents. "I'm sorry, Cassie. That's got to be tough."

"I manage." She surveyed the room and smiled, although it didn't quite reach her eyes. "I love this place. It's so chic. And it beats the heck out of the hospital cafeteria."

She laid a cheek on her palm. He focused on her long delicate fingers capped with neat red-painted nails. He remembered those fingers well, how she had touched him. His reaction was immediate, swift, unexpected.

Shifting in his seat, he picked up the menu. "What are you in the mood for?" He knew exactly what he was in the mood for, and he wouldn't find it on the menu.

She nibbled her bottom lip as she looked over the menu once again. "Nothing too heavy. Or too spicy."

Spicy was foremost on Brendan's mind. "The stuffed snapper is good."

"True. I've had it before. But I'm thinking pasta with some decadent cream sauce."

Decadent would definitely describe Brendan's sudden craving for Cassie. "I'm going to have the filet. Medium rare."

Cassie wrinkled her nose. "I don't do beef."

Man, she'd stepped right into that one. "What else don't you do?"

She grinned. "Wouldn't you like to know?"

Oh, yeah, he would, and right now. It took all his strength not to forget dinner, take her out of here and kiss her senseless. Show her the pleasure he'd failed to show her that fateful night that had brought them to this point.

The waiter stopped by, interrupting the moment. The guy couldn't seem to keep his eyes off Cassie, and that bugged the hell out of Brendan. The jerk took their order and took his leave before Brendan gave in to the urge to punch him.

While they waited on the food, they talked about the Neelys' little girl, Cassie's frustration over being overworked, all the while avoiding the issue at hand—their future.

The food came quickly, and they ate in silence while Brendan tried to prepare for what would come after the meal. Once they were done, they both turned down dessert. Someone must have turned up the heat, Brendan thought. Right now he was sweating without mercy.

Cassie regarded him with a steady stare. "Well?"

"Well what?"

"Don't you have something to ask me?"

He did, but the words stuck in his throat. Taking in a deep draw of air, he gathered his thoughts. "Have you made a decision?"

Cassie took the cloth napkin she'd been folding and put it in a chokehold. "Actually, I have."

Brendan's chest tightened with fear. Fear she might say yes, because he wasn't sure he could be the man she needed. Fear she would say no, because he knew it was the right thing to do. "What did you decide?"

She tossed the napkin aside and straightened. "I've decided that what you said is true. Life is all about risks. Nothing's a guarantee. And besides—" her smile came back into play "—it would be so much fun to be able to harass you on a daily basis."

Brendan released the breath he hadn't realized he'd been holding. "So is that a yes?"

"Yes, it's a yes. I will marry you, Brendan O'Connor."

He tried to take her hand but she yanked it back, her expression suddenly solemn. "But," she said, "you have to promise me that we'll always be honest with each other."

"We always have been." At least with most things. Brendan had yet to tell her about his son.

Someday he would, when he felt he could—after
their baby was born, safe and healthy. And he would
do everything in his power to make sure that happened this time.

"Are you through?" he asked.

"Yes, I guess so."

"Then let's get out of here." He stood and tossed
a hundred-dollar bill on the table.

Cassie stared at the money, mouth gaping. "I
don't think we ate that much, Brendan."

"The guy deserves a tip for his speedy service.
He deserved a belt in his gut for staring at you all
night." God, he sounded like a jealous fool.

Cassie sent him a knowing smile. "He's a hunk,
all right. If you're into pale, skeletal men."

Brendan took Cassie's hand and led her out of the
restaurant, surprised at how natural it felt. But when
they reached Cassie's car, they stood face-to-face in
awkward silence.

Brendan wasn't sure what to do next. This change
in their relationship had him off balance. A few
months ago, they would have parted with nothing
more than a friendly goodbye. But now Brendan
didn't want a simple goodbye. He wanted her. That
much he couldn't deny, no matter what the future
held for them. He also didn't want her to think that
that's all he wanted.

Restraint wasn't always a virtue he possessed, at
least where women were concerned. But Cassie
wasn't anything like the other women he had
known. She was a confidante, a friend, and soon to
be his wife. The mother of his child. That thought
gave him pause, and another sting of nervousness.

Cassie regarded him with an expectant look. He

answered it by saying, "I really enjoyed this evening," as if becoming officially engaged was nothing more than your average mating ritual.

"I assume the evening's over then?" she asked with a good measure of disappointment.

"Actually, I think we need to take a few minutes to talk about our plans."

Cassie shivered. "It's getting cold out here. Mind if we talk in the car?"

"Sure." The car would provide some warmth, not that Brendan needed any. He did need to keep a lid on his urges.

She tripped the lock with her key then walked to the driver's side while he opened the passenger door and slid in. The aged sedan was larger than most with a bench seat, not buckets, but Brendan felt as if his knees were attached to his chest.

"Can you put the seat back?" he asked once she was settled behind the wheel.

"Okeydokey." She reached beneath her and pulled the bar, sending the seat back in a rush. She giggled. "Did I give you whiplash?"

"My neck's okay." Some of his parts were anything but okay with Cassie sitting there in that dress, looking made for sin, smelling like a garden. For God's sake, she was pregnant. He had to remember that.

Cassie flipped the center armrest up. "Do you care if I come over there?"

Yeah, he cared. If she came any closer, he might lose control. If he said no, he might hurt her feelings. Patting the seat beside him, he said, "Sure. Come on."

With a satisfied smile she slid toward him. Too

close to offer him much comfort. He draped his arm over the back of the seat and shifted sideways to gain a little distance.

"Don't look so serious, Brendan," she said. "Getting married isn't a death sentence. You need to relax."

Relax? He couldn't relax, not with her so near. "Maybe we should talk about the wedding." Not a bad idea, although at the moment he could only think about the honeymoon.

"Okay. When should we do it?"

"Do what?"

"Get married."

That word clamped his gut in a vise. "I'll be working nights starting tomorrow. Segovia's going on vacation for three weeks."

Cassie frowned. "Three weeks?"

"Yeah. I'll be working the usual twelve-hour shift. Albers will be filling in and since he's the chief, he gets the day shift." He rubbed a hand over his chin. "But since I'll be off during the day, we could pick an afternoon next week to go down to the courthouse."

She lowered her eyes to her lap. "I guess we could do that."

Brendan felt like a certified jerk for not considering what Cassie might want. "Unless you'd rather wait and have a bigger wedding to include your family."

She raised sad eyes to him. "Other than my dad, I don't have any family. What about you?"

"Actually, my mom and dad are retired. They travel a lot. I'm not sure exactly where they are at the moment, somewhere in Europe. They're not due back until Christmas.''

"We really can't wait until Christmas. I'll be showing by then.''

She had a point there, Brendan decided. "Then it's just you and me.''

"And the Kempners," she added. "I thought I'd ask Michelle and Nick to be our witnesses, if that's okay with you. Unless you have someone else in mind.''

"Not really. I don't know Nick all that well, but he seems like a good guy.''

"He is.'' Cassie chewed her bottom lip. "So it's settled, then. We'll do it one afternoon next week at the courthouse.''

Brendan tipped her chin up to look at him. "I'm sorry Cassie. I know this probably isn't what you envisioned when you thought about getting married.''

She shrugged. "I rarely thought about getting married, so rest assured, you're not bursting my proverbial bubble.''

Brendan sensed he was failing miserably at giving her what she needed. He brought his arm around her, and she laid her head against his shoulder. The feel of her snuggled against him in the solitude of the car brought back the desire he couldn't seem to stop. He pulled her closer.

"I'm also sorry I didn't buy you a ring. I wasn't sure what your answer would be, and there wasn't enough time.''

She raised her head and smiled. "I don't need a diamond, if that's what you're thinking. Besides, it would only get in the way when we play tennis.''

"Now that you're pregnant, looks like that's going to come to an end for a while."

"Why?"

"Because you need to take care of yourself and the baby."

She released a frustrated sigh. "Brendan, I'm not fragile. Besides, exercise is good for the baby."

Brendan couldn't get a handle on his concern. "To a point."

"I'll talk to the doctor about it."

"Have you made an appointment yet?"

"Yes. Dr. Anderson will see me in two weeks."

That wasn't good enough, in Brendan's opinion. Not where his child was concerned. "I'll call him and try to get you in sooner."

"Would you stop worrying? Nothing will happen in two weeks' time. I haven't even had any morning sickness."

In his rational mind, he knew she was probably right, nothing would happen. But the anxiety wouldn't let up. "Humor me, okay?"

"If I must." She stroked her knuckles over his jaw, sending a skein of pleasure down his spine. "I can tell I've got my work cut out for me, trying to keep you from going crazy over the next six months."

She was driving him crazy now, to the point of total distraction. As if she'd decided to conduct a test of his willpower, Cassie kissed him. A bold uninhibited kiss that had her taking the lead in a meeting of lips and tongues, sending Brendan hurtling headlong into desire.

Needing her closer, he lifted her legs and brought them to rest on his thighs, curving his hand on the swell of her bottom. The satin felt cool beneath his palms, but his body suffered a sudden three-alarm blaze.

He broke the kiss to regain his bearings. If he didn't, he was in danger of initiating Cassie's car. But he couldn't seem to move his hand from the smooth contours of her hip.

"What are you wearing underneath this dress?" he asked.

She smiled up at him. "Basically a kite string attached to a patch of satin."

"Huh?"

"A thong. Prevents panty lines."

And encourages the libido, Brendan decided. "Really? Sounds interesting."

"Maybe." She sounded winded, excited. "If you appreciate that kind of thing."

Oh, he appreciated it all right. Too much.

Clinging to only a modicum of restraint, he kissed her again. It took all his strength not to lay her down on the seat. Her mouth was soft, pliant. So was she, perfectly tucked in his arms. Warm, soft, his. At least for a few more moments.

Brendan's hand traveled across her thigh slowly, meeting the place where the dress ended and silk-covered flesh began. He continued underneath her hem, wanting to please her, to appease his desperate need to touch her.

In the far reaches of his rational mind, Brendan knew he should stop. He wasn't a kid anymore, when a back seat had been all that was available to him. Cassie deserved more than quick roll in a car.

But when he tried to move his hand away, her legs parted, giving him room to explore. He took advantage of the situation, working his way up to his ultimate destination.

Cassie heard bells, and Brendan hadn't even really touched her yet, at least not in the way she wanted. When she heard the ringing again, she suddenly realized it was the annoying shrill of a cellular phone. Brendan's phone. She reluctantly scooted off his lap and laid her head back on the seat, trying to regain normal respiration.

Brendan groaned and leaned his forehead against the dashboard. He reached behind him and took the phone from its holder attached to his belt beneath his jacket. "What!"

Cassie pitied the recipient of Brendan's hostility. She couldn't blame him, though. She was feeling a bit out of sorts over the interruption.

"Yeah, this is Dr. O'Connor." He leaned back and closed his eyes. "Okay. I'll be there in ten minutes."

He replaced the phone and turned his head toward Cassie. "Are you okay?"

No, she wasn't. She was frustrated and keyed up, ready to tackle him and make him finish what he'd started. "I'm just wonderful," she said through gritted teeth.

"I didn't exactly plan this," he said.

"I understand, Brendan. Duty calls."

"Not the phone call. I meant getting carried away. I think it was that discussion about your underwear."

One more minute and he would have gotten to know her underwear personally, along with everything beneath it. Darn the hospital. "Just goes to

show that the best things in life are sometimes un-
planned."

His expression turned serious once again. "I have
to go in to the unit."

Cassie straightened and tugged down the hem of
her dress. "I assumed that. Problems?"

"Triplets."

"Wow."

He smiled. "You can say that again. I can't imagine having more than one to deal with, much less
three."

She wouldn't mind at all. "I guess some people
are better equipped to deal with it."

He took her hand into his. "I'll call you tomorrow. We can get the license at lunch, then get married next Tuesday. How does that sound?"

That didn't give her much time to plan, but after
all, it would be a simple ceremony. No big deal. No
fancy dress required. Nothing more than making it
official. And that made her somewhat sad. "Sounds
like a winner."

"Since it looks like I'll be pulling a double,
maybe more than one, I might not see you much
before then. I'm on all weekend. It's going to be
crazy with Segovia out."

Disappointment filled Cassie, but she didn't intend to whine about it. Such was a doctor's life, and
she was about to enter the world of a doctor's wife.
She might as well get used to the crazy hours. She
didn't have to like it, though. "Okay. Just touch
base with me now and then, okay?"

"Okay." He leaned over and brushed a kiss on
her cheek. "Get some sleep. One of us needs to."

She probably wouldn't sleep at all, but she didn't

dare tell him that. Cupping his jaw with her palm, she said, "Thank you, Brendan. For everything."

His smile resurfaced. "Next time, I'll turn off the damned phone." Then he was gone in a flash, out the car door before Cassie could blink.

Watching him walk into the shadows toward his own car, Cassie clung to the promise of "next time." She couldn't help but wish for different circumstances. Wished that she could spend tonight in his arms, shutting out the world. No need to waste energy hoping for something that wasn't possible, at least not at the moment. But after they were married, anything was possible. At least she'd have him all to herself, when she wasn't sharing him with the hospital.

One thing Cassie was quickly learning—Brendan wanted her, at least from a physical standpoint. In order to get his attention, all she had to do was give him a little encouragement. And maybe, just maybe, that might be enough to bring him around.

Maybe by loving him enough, he might eventually love her back.

Five

"**Y**ou're getting what?"

Cassie regarded Michelle Kempner's stunned expression over the breakfast nook in her friend's kitchen, wondering exactly how much she should reveal about the circumstances behind the sudden nuptials.

"I said I'm getting married," Cassie repeated.

"You told Nick and me that you didn't have any prospects." Michelle put up a hand to stop Cassie's response. "No, wait, let me guess. The groom wouldn't happen to be a gorgeous doctor by the name of Brendan O'Connor, would it?"

Cassie's mouth dropped open. "How would you know that?"

Michelle rolled her eyes. "Come on, Cassie. Everyone at the hospital knows you two are an item. You leave together almost all the time. You have lunch together in the cafeteria. I've always suspected there was something brewing between you two. I'm just hurt you never told me how close you'd become.''

If Michelle only knew, Cassie thought.

A clatter of pots and pans drew Michelle and Cassie's attention to the kitchen floor where Michelle's five-year-old stepdaughter sat raiding the cabinets.

"Kelsey, honey," Michelle said. "Would you like to go watch a video until Daddy gets home?''

Kelsey yawned and stretched, then nodded her head. "Can we watch the one with the skating bear?''

Michelle stood and lifted Kelsey from the floor by her arms, then swung her around, sending the little girl into a fit of giggles. "Okay, the bear it is. But you have to watch it by yourself for a little while. I need to talk to my friend.''

Kelsey eyed Cassie with impatience, then gave her cherub smile to Michelle. "'Kay, Shelly. You can talk for a little while.''

Michelle touched the end of Kelsey's upturned nose and smiled. "Well, thank you, missy, for giving me your permission.'' She grabbed Kelsey up into her arms and told Cassie, "I'll be back in a minute. She'll probably take an *n-a-p*.''

"I'm not sleepy," Kelsey said with determination on the way out of the kitchen.

Cassie settled back in the chair with her cup of tea, thinking she would love to have a little girl like Kelsey. Or a boy would be fine, too. Whatever the gender, she would cherish her child, give it all that it needed. Her baby would never feel as if it were invisible and insignificant.

Michelle returned and sat back down at the table. "So, give me details."

Cassie's gaze slid away. "We plan to have the ceremony next Tuesday. At the courthouse." She turned her attention back to Michelle. "I'd like you and Nick to be our witnesses."

"We'd love to, if you'll explain why the hurry."

Drawing in a long breath, Cassie geared up to tell Michelle everything. "Actually, I'm pregnant."

"You're kidding."

Cassie rimmed a finger over her teacup, avoiding Michelle's steady scrutiny. "No, I'm not."

"How did that happen?"

"The usual way."

Michelle laughed. "I'm sorry, I'm just surprised. But I guess nothing's fool-proof, right?"

"It was only one time."

"One time?"

"Yes, only one time." And nothing had happened since.

Michelle pinned Cassie with a hard stare. "You sound sad. What's wrong?"

Cassie wasn't sure how much to divulge about her relationship with Brendan, but right now she was dying inside over the fact that he didn't love her, beyond the love for a friend. "Nothing's wrong, really. It's just that this thing between Brendan and me happened so fast. And now there's a baby to consider, and I don't know how he really feels...." Too much information, Cassie decided.

"You don't know how he feels about the baby or you?" Michelle asked in an understanding tone.

Cassie could use a good soul cleansing. She could trust Michelle not to pass judgment, only to listen.

"How he feels about me. Up to this point, we've been only good friends. Brendan was having a tough time one night, problems at work, and one thing led to another and I got pregnant."

Michelle laid a gentle hand on Cassie's arm. "You're in love with him." It wasn't a question.

"Yes, I guess I am. But I'm afraid he doesn't feel the same about me. Or if he does, he's never said."

"Have you told him how you feel?"

"No. Not yet. I don't want to scare him off. He's had enough to deal with."

"Give him time, Cassie. You know how some men are. The less said, the better they feel. Some just can't acknowledge those emotions."

"Was Nick that way?"

Michelle threaded her bottom lip through her teeth, looking hesitant. "Actually, Nick told me he loved me before I ever told him. But everyone's different."

Cassie couldn't agree more. Brendan was different from any man she had known, in some very positive ways. Still, she had her concerns that he might never feel the same about her as she did for him. She would have to take the chance that his feelings would change with time. She had no choice.

Cassie tried to smile. "Regardless of what happens between Brendan and me, our baby will be loved by us both."

Michelle sent her a kind smile. "Don't give up on him, Cassie. Sometimes fortitude is your greatest friend."

But with Brendan's guarded nature, would it be Cassie's greatest foe?

* * *

It had been an uneventful wedding, at least for Cassie. Four hours ago she and Brendan had left the courthouse dressed in their Sunday best, sporting plain gold bands and carrying a license that proclaimed they were married. The justice of the peace had rushed through the ceremony at breakneck speed, probably because it had been nearing lunchtime. Michelle and Nick had fulfilled their duties as witnesses, but Cassie sensed they'd been uncomfortable with the obligation. The couple had taken off after polite congratulations immediately following Brendan's requisite kiss, leaving Cassie to ponder if she had done the right thing.

Now she stood in her living room, surveying the boxes Brendan was bringing in from the car. They had decided that her house was better suited for their new life together, especially since Brendan's apartment had only one bedroom.

Cassie couldn't help but wonder if Brendan planned to stay in her spare bedroom until the baby was born. He'd never said that, but right now she was feeling anything but confident.

Walking to the middle of the room, she picked up one box marked Clothes, intending to carry it to her bedroom to let him know he was welcome there. But she stopped short when she noted the animal-print underwear peeking out from beneath the stack of briefs.

Tucking the small box under her arm, she pulled the garment out, relieved it wasn't a pair of panties. Nope, they were briefs. Bikini briefs, very brief, meant to be worn by a man. But Brendan?

She held them up pinched between her forefinger and thumb and giggled.

"Those were given to me."

Cassie looked from the briefs to Brendan now standing at the doorway, holding a TV. He didn't look at all happy over her intrusion into his privacy.

She couldn't stop her grin. "They kind of caught my attention." If he wore them that would certainly keep her attention.

Placing the TV on the floor in front of the sofa, Brendan strode to her. She backed up, still dangling the briefs.

"Well, Tarzan, I'm shocked. I didn't know you had such exotic tastes."

He crooked a finger at her. "Hand 'em over, Cassie."

She slid the box to the floor and held the bikinis up with both hands. "Hmmm...leopard print. I would've taken you for the tiger type."

He took two more steps. "It was a joke."

She didn't consider them to be at all funny, not with the image of Brendan wearing them branding her brain. "So they have sentimental value?"

"No. I just haven't bothered to throw them away." He tried to snatch them from her, but she quickly moved back, landing against the wall. She hid the briefs behind her. "Say please, Doctor."

Without a word, he slid his arms around her. Trapped, and she loved it.

"Turnabout is fair play," he said, his voice low and husky. "Now you have to show me your underwear."

She'd tried that in the car last week, without success. But maybe now he might be willing to take a better look. She glanced down at her ragged sweats, the only thing that fit since her jeans were already too tight. "My hands are occupied at the moment, but feel free to explore."

He visually followed the path her gaze had taken, but much more slowly. After a time, he brought his eyes back to hers. "Sounds like a great idea, but I have to leave for work in thirty minutes. Maybe later?"

Later meant *who knew when,* and Cassie wasn't sure she could wait. She wriggled her arms from beneath his and stuffed the briefs in his back pocket, then grabbed his belt loops to tug him closer. Very close. Not even an inch separated them. She could feel every part of him, including the hard ridge pressed against her belly. Let the honeymoon begin.

Standing on tiptoes, Cassie brought her lips to his and delivered a soft kiss. A kiss meant to tease, to taunt. From the smoldering look in Brendan's eyes, she suspected it was working. "You know, we don't need that much time." She pulled his arms around her waist and rested his hands on her hips.

Lifting his shirt, she placed a kiss on his sternum. She relished the taste of salt on his skin and the trace scent of his cologne. "Are you sure I can't interest you in a quickie?"

"Hell, no, I'm not sure. But I'm not going to change my mind. I want to be able to take my time." He tipped her chin up, forcing her to look at him. "I want to make love to you in a bed, not up against a wall."

The thought of him taking her up against a wall sent shivers all over Cassie's body. "What's wrong with the wall?"

"Under normal circumstances, not a damn thing.

But you're pregnant. I'm not going to do anything that might hurt you.''

The man was frustrating her beyond belief with his insistence that she was some flimsy, wilting flower. For goodness' sake, she was an athlete. ''Brendan, you're being ridiculous. Pregnant women make love all the time.''

He surveyed her face, from forehead to chin before bringing his gaze back to her eyes. ''I know they do, and I know that's what you want. But I also know that I have to be careful with you this time.''

She didn't want careful. She wanted hot, lusty sex. Obviously her hormones were in an uproar. Or maybe it was simply the idea of making love with Brendan. *Really* making love.

Disregarding his concern, she kissed him again, this time not so gently. And he responded with an impatient, needy groan. But he took what she willingly gave, meeting her tongue stroke for stroke. He was flush against her, stealing her breath, stoking her desire. His hand slipped under her T-shirt to cup her breast through cotton; her hand went to the snap on his fly. He slid his hand down to the obvious curve of her belly…

And suddenly his hand was no longer there. She felt bereft, and thoroughly disappointed over the loss.

Putting more distance between them, he tugged on his ear and sighed. ''You're going to do me in, did you know that?''

She crossed her arms over her chest. ''I hope so.''

He redid his fly. ''I guess you know what's going to happen now, don't you?''

"You're going to take me to bed and have your way with me?" she asked hopefully.

"First, I'm going to take a shower. Alone or I'll be late to work."

Cassie stuck out her lip in a pout. "You're no fun."

"Second," he continued. "I'm going to walk around the unit all night long hard as steel trying to hide behind anything available so I don't lose my dignity in front of my staff."

Cassie grinned and sauntered over to him. "You know, I could take care of that for you."

He clasped her wrist before she could act on her impulse and brought her palm to his lips. "I'll manage until tomorrow morning."

"I have to be at work in the morning. I'll probably be leaving before you get home."

"Then I'll try to be back early."

"And if you're not?"

"Maybe we can meet in one of the on-call rooms at the hospital."

She scowled. "Some honeymoon."

He bracketed her face in his palms and touched his forehead to hers. "I'm sorry, Cassie. First that lousy excuse for a wedding, and now this. I'll try to make it up to you soon. Maybe we can take a trip in the next few weeks, at least before the baby's born."

She didn't care about a trip. She only wanted to be with him now. They could make love anywhere. In the bed. On the sofa. Up against the wall. It didn't matter, as long as they did make love, consummate the marriage. Only then would it become real to Cassie.

* * *

But it didn't happen the next day, or the next. When Brendan was at work, Cassie was at home sleeping, and vice versa. Instead of ending his shift earlier, he'd worked late both days.

And Cassie was miserable.

Speaking to Brendan periodically by phone, hearing his constant apologies for being absent in her life, even his assurances that he would get a day off soon, hadn't appeased her need to be with him in every sense of the word. But that didn't mean she couldn't do something about it. She considered herself a proactive person, exactly what drove her to her current plan. A plan that had formed while considering Brendan's suggestion that they utilize an on-call room. A plan, if executed properly, that would put an end to her frustration, at least for a while.

Cassie waited until everyone had left the department to transform her office into a romantic den of iniquity. She'd already put her colleagues in an uproar when she'd announced that Brendan O'Connor had married her. She certainly didn't want to risk anyone catching her with her pants down in her workplace.

She draped a white lace cloth over her desk, placed two candles in the center along with the take-out Chinese food she'd had delivered, and sprinkled some musky potpourri into a glass bowl on the end table next to the small love seat. She laid a thick blue blanket on the floor between her desk and the sofa along with two satin-covered feather pillows. Not much room to roam, but adequate space for two people in the throes of passion.

Now all she needed was Brendan.

Glancing at the clock, she only had a few more minutes to put the final touches on her preparation. Brendan had promised to meet her for dinner in the cafeteria at 8:00 p.m. She'd left word with a unit clerk that she would meet him in her office instead. Boy, was he in for a surprise.

Cassie walked into the adjacent bathroom joining the two neighboring offices, stripped out of her clothes and slipped on a peach-colored short silk gown with matching robe. After applying a subtle hint of perfume, she strolled back in the room on bare feet, sat on the sofa, and waited.

The minutes ticked off slowly, left behind by her sprinting pulse. What if he didn't get the message? What if he went to the cafeteria, didn't find her there then went back to work? What if the janitorial staff found her sitting half-naked, needy and alone?

She certainly couldn't worry about that. Besides, she planned to bolt the door as soon as Brendan arrived. *If* he arrived.

Cassie was beginning to believe that might not happen when the knock came at the door. She rose on shaky knees and answered the summons, hoping it was Brendan and not some secretary burning the midnight oil.

"Sorry I'm late, but—" Brendan's words cut off when he took in Cassie's suggestive apparel.

Cassie decided she could drop a two-pointer with a golf ball into his open mouth. She'd rather kiss him.

Instead, she pulled him inside and tripped the lock on the door, then leaned back against it. "Honeymoon on wheels, at your service. If this works out, I might go into business for myself.''

Brendan surveyed the office, then faced her, no less shocked. ''How long have you been planning this?''

''Since yesterday, when I realized we might not ever be alone again. I decided to improvise.''

His gaze traveled to the makeshift bed on the floor. ''I see you've thought of everything.''

''Uh-huh. Are you surprised?''

''Yeah. I am.''

Cassie approached him slowly and placed her hands on his shoulders. Nodding toward the desk, she said, ''I've got your favorite, beef and broccoli with a few egg rolls thrown in.''

He glanced at the food. ''Pretty creative, Cassie Allen.''

She tried to tamp down the sudden hurt. ''That's Cassie O'Connor to you, Doctor.''

He revealed a weak smile. ''Oh, yeah. I forgot.''

She was determined to make him remember that—and many things—before the evening ended.

Brendan glanced at his watch. ''I have about thirty minutes before I have to be back.''

Plenty of time, Cassie decided. Especially if they skipped dinner. Brendan had other ideas.

''Okay,'' he said. ''Let's eat.''

Resigned to the fact that her most important plan would have to wait, Cassie joined him at the desk where they sat across from each other. She filled their plates and poured them both a glass of soda, all the while thinking that she didn't want the darned food. Her hunger existed on a deeper level, a hunger than only Brendan could satisfy.

"Sorry I don't have any wine," she said, trying to sound cheerful. "But with you working and me pregnant, I decided we'd have to forgo that pleasure." She heavily emphasized *that pleasure* to let him know she had other pleasurable things in store for him later.

As they ate, Brendan seemed preoccupied, almost nervous. He didn't say that much, only responded with brief answers when Cassie asked him questions about his evening.

Cassie finally gave up on conversation and chose to concentrate on eating. She noticed immediately that Brendan occasionally glanced at her mouth, as if he found it fascinating. And when the robe slipped off her shoulder, his gaze came to rest there. She didn't bother to readjust, realizing that maybe the good doctor might be more than willing to have a little post-dinner playtime. And she would use that to her advantage.

Cassie attempted her best techniques of seduction, occasionally licking her lips, brushing Brendan's hand when she reached for a napkin, anything to let him subtly know exactly what she wanted. As best she could tell, she'd been successful. Brendan's eyes began to darken to a deeper green, and he shifted in his seat more than once.

By the end of the meal, the tension had increased—as overt as the scent of potpourri and the aroma of the pungent food.

Brendan pushed his plate back, the food only half-eaten. "I'm done."

Cassie wasn't done at all, at least not with Brendan.

She picked up a plastic-wrapped cookie. "Would you like to read your fortune?"

He smiled. "You can do it for me. You always do."

Cassie worked the covering away and snapped the cookie in two then withdrew the slender paper. "It says 'Be satisfied in all that you endeavor.'" She looked up with a grin. "Sounds like good advice to me."

With that, she stood and moved around the desk to face Brendan. "Why don't we try a little satisfaction?"

Not giving him a chance to respond, Cassie pulled Brendan up and led him to the small sofa. She nudged him down on the edge then stood before him and slipped the robe off her shoulders, leaving her clad in nothing more than the short nightie and a smile.

Brendan took a long visual expedition down her body, his gaze coming to rest on her expanding abdomen outlined by the sheer material. She resisted the urge to cover her belly with both hands.

When Brendan continued to stare, Cassie's insecurities surfaced. "I know. I'm getting fat."

He braced his hands on her sides and pulled her forward, then placed a gentle kiss on her tummy. "I think it's great."

At least he cared about their child, but how much did he care about her? Cassie wouldn't let herself think about that now. Not while she had so little time left.

Brendan rested his forehead against her middle, his hands gripped tightly on her hips.

She placed her palms on the crown of his head

then slid them to his shoulders, immediately noticing the faint tremors beneath her fingers. "You're shaking."

"I know."

"Are you cold?"

"Not even close."

Deciding to turn up the heat even more, Cassie stepped back and lowered the straps from the gown, letting it slink to the floor in a pool of silk. She was completely naked now, yet Brendan only stared without speaking or moving. When he caught her gaze, she detected a trace of desire in his eyes and knew she had succeeded in getting his attention, but he looked hesitant.

"Brendan, I know you're uncomfortable with this, but I need—"

"I know what you need." His tone was low, coarse, compelling.

When he took her hand and brought her down on the sofa beside him, Cassie grabbed for the drawstring on his scrubs. He stopped her with a hand on her wrist. "Not this time, Cassie." His strained voice hinted at his struggle for control.

Bringing her legs to rest in his lap, much the same as he'd done in the car, he sent his hands and his mouth on a journey over her naked body. He worked her breast lightly with the tip of his tongue while palming her waist, then her hip before moving gentle fingertips to the inside of her thigh. His touch was leisurely, pure velvet, soft yet insistent as he made his way up, up, setting the stage for sweet surrender. She moaned when his expert fingers whispered over intimate flesh. She gasped when he centered on the heart of her need. She buried her face in his neck as he played her with tender strokes.

Never had anyone taken such care to tend her needs. Never had she emotionally offered herself so freely to any man. Never had she wanted so much, needed so much.

Brendan's capable hand reduced her to nothing more than soul-stirring sensation. Her breath came in short puffs of air as she moved closer and closer to release. Tension coiled beneath his skilled fingertips. As Brendan had only moments before, she began to tremble, mildly aware that his hold on her tightened, but he didn't let up with the sensual onslaught. With sultry words he persuaded her, guided her past the point of thought. All too soon she gave in to the climax that shook her to the core and took her to a realm of pleasure that she'd never visited before now. Before Brendan.

Brendan continued to hold her close while painting soft kisses on her neck, her jaw, her lips. Her body still hummed with aftershocks of fulfillment, but the deep-rooted need didn't subside. Only one thing would make this moment perfect…and the sudden offensive noise in the hallway wasn't it.

The drone of a vacuum coming from nearby signaled the custodian's arrival and cut into Cassie's euphoria. She raised her head when Brendan tensed, his attention now focused on the closed door.

"Damn." His tone was a frustrated as Cassie felt.

She cupped his jaw and brought his face back to her. "It's locked," she whispered.

He expelled a rough sigh. "They have a key."

Cassie realized he was probably right, but she

wasn't ready for their time together to end. Obviously, Brendan was.

Carefully moving her aside, he rose from the couch, picked up her robe from the floor and offered it to her. "You might want to put this on just in case."

She reluctantly complied, wanting badly to cry and throw a tantrum over the untimely interruption. Instead she stood, feeling cold and lonely even though she was now completely covered and Brendan was still present.

"Are you sure we can't continue this?" she asked in a voice that bordered on pleading. "They probably won't get to this office for at least another fifteen minutes."

"I'm not willing to chance that. Besides, the way I'm feeling now, I'd probably be too rough on you."

Cassie rolled her eyes. "I'm pregnant, Brendan, not an invalid."

"I realize that, but I don't want to hurt you."

He was hurting her now by leaving her without the prospect of making this marriage real in every sense of the word.

Again he consulted his watch. "I've got to get back. I'm going to be late if I don't."

Cassie tried to smile, but her lips felt stiff with the effort. "You hardly ate anything."

"Take it home. I'll have it for breakfast."

Cassie's stomach pitched at the thought. "Okay." She hugged her arms to her middle. "So much for the honeymoon."

Brendan brought her against his solid chest and brushed a kiss over her forehead. "I'm sorry, Cassie. Seems like nothing's gone right lately."

She pulled back and studied his solemn expression. "I would have to argue that. You did everything right a few minutes ago."

He sighed. "It's not enough. This isn't fair to you, the little bit of time we have together. And I don't see it coming to an end anytime soon."

"I'm okay." She sent a pointed look down at some pretty strong evidence that he needed attention. "You're not okay."

"I'm fine."

She met his gaze. "You're lying."

He reluctantly grinned. "Yeah, well, I've been in worse shape before."

She decided not to argue the point. He was obviously determined to ignore his own needs.

"By the way," she said, "the doctor's office called and they moved my appointment to tomorrow at 10 a.m. Did you happen to have anything to do with that?"

"Like I told you, I didn't want you to have to wait. Early prenatal care is very important." He sounded like the doctor, not the husband.

Cassie posed the next question at the risk of his rejection. "Do you want to come with me? I mean, I know you'll be asleep, so you don't have to—"

"I can catch a couple of hours, then meet you there."

Relieved and thrilled, Cassie said, "Great. I'll set the alarm before I leave for work."

"Now that that's settled, I need to get back to the unit." He headed to the adjacent bathroom, leaving Cassie alone with her disappointment. But at least he'd agreed to go to the appointment with her. That was something. Maybe Dr. Anderson would assure him that making love wasn't taboo during pregnancy. At least Cassie could hope it would be enough to convince Brendan that she didn't need to be handled like fine china. Convince him that they could be good together, if only given the chance.

Brendan surfaced a few moments later, the hair at his forehead damp as if he'd thrown water in his face. He probably had. She managed a smile although she was more than a little annoyed that he had to leave so quickly, even though in her logical mind she knew he needed to get back to work.

He hugged her, kissed her lightly on the lips and headed to the door. "Thanks for dinner. I'll see you at home."

She raised her hand to wave. "Yeah. I hope. Someday."

Brendan left Cassie with a weak smile, cold Chinese food, a makeshift unused bed as a reminder of her failure along with a melancholy mood she couldn't shake.

Although Brendan had shown her perfect pleasure, she still hadn't received what she needed from him—either physically or emotionally. She wondered if she ever would.

Something kept him at a distance. Something personal that he'd buried deep below the calm facade.

Cassie would have to find out more, and soon, if she ever hoped to scale the wall he'd so effectively built around his heart. In the meantime she would have to be patient until he finally came around. *If* he came around.

Once again, as it had been most of her life, loneliness was Cassie's only companion, and hope was all that she had to hold on to.

Six

He hadn't been this frustrated in years.

Just as well they had been interrupted, Brendan decided. What he'd said to Cassie a few hours before had been the absolute truth. If they had continued, he would have had a difficult time being careful with her. And he had to be careful. Very careful. He wouldn't do anything to risk hurting either Cassie or their baby.

Unfortunately, he had hurt Cassie on more than one occasion, and he hated that he couldn't give her everything she needed. But he had to quit thinking about that now, about everything, about what might have been. If he didn't, he wouldn't be any good to anyone. Especially not his patients who waited for him down the hall.

"Dr. O'Connor, are you okay?"

Brendan looked up from his second cup of coffee

to Millie Myers standing in the break room door, a hospital fixture with twenty years tenure. She had a way with sick babies and a wit that could rust stainless steel. She also had a penchant for mothering the younger doctors, and Brendan was no exception. Right now he didn't need a mother, but he had a feeling he was going to get one, anyway.

Sprigs of gray hair trailed from beneath the blue cap resting crooked atop Millie's head, her tired blue eyes reflecting her concern. She looked wrung-out, done in, and she was asking him if he was okay? Considering the rough night they'd had on the unit so far, everyone ought to look frazzled. And they still had another eight hours to go.

Brendan sat forward, laced his hands behind his neck and stretched. "I'm fine, Millie. Just taking a break. What's up?"

Millie shuffled to the counter, one palm braced on the small of her back. "The hydrocephalic baby's on his way down from the shunt repair."

"His name?"

"I'm not sure."

Anger pierced through the fog of his exhaustion. Every child had an identity. *Every* child, even those who might not stand a chance at survival. "He's got a name, Millie. He's not just the 'hydrocephalic baby.'"

Millie frowned. "Calm down, okay? I'll find out before he arrives on the unit."

He lowered his voice and sent her an apologetic look. "Sorry. I'm beat. How long before he's here?"

"They said another fifteen minutes."

Fifteen minutes probably wouldn't be enough

time for the caffeine to kick in, under normal circumstances. Truth was, Brendan didn't really need any more stimulation. Cassie had provided that with her spontaneous "dinner." He still hadn't come down from the sexual high, still keyed up to the point of total turmoil.

Millie joined him at the table, pulled back a chair and collapsed into it. "By the way, I've been meaning to tell you congratulations on your marriage. Cassie's a great girl."

How well Brendan knew that. "Yeah. She's the best."

Silent and solemn, Millie continued to stare at Brendan until he finally had enough of her scrutiny. "Is there a problem, Millie?"

"No problem with me. What about you?"

Brendan propped his elbows on the table and forked both hands through his hair. "Nothing a little sleep wouldn't cure."

"Or maybe a little activity between the sheets?" Millie's ensuing laugh sounded like sandpaper on bricks.

Brendan couldn't help the wry smile that formed, even though he didn't feel like smiling. "You're a wicked, wicked woman, Millie Beth."

She responded with a wily grin. "And a wise woman, don't forget that. I've been married for thirty years to the same man and I know that look when I see it. The one that says, Take me now, I'm about to blow."

Brendan grumbled, not daring to admit she was right. He wrapped his hands around the mug and stared into the cup to avoid her perceptive eyes. "Whatever you say, Millie."

"I also say you need to take some time off to be with that pretty wife of yours."

"I can't right now. We're short on staff."

"Bull. Need I remind you that life is short?"

No one needed to remind him of that. He dealt with the reality every day. "Time to get back to work."

"Just one more question, Doctor. Now I know this is probably none of my business—"

"Then don't ask," Brendan warned, but to no avail.

"Is there a possibility that the reason behind you finally taking the marriage plunge has something to do with you becoming a daddy?"

Brendan's gaze shot from the coffee cup to Millie. "Who told you that?"

"Remember, I've also had four kids. I saw Cassie yesterday. Either she's got a cushion stuffed up her blouse, or she has a bun in the oven."

He, too, had noticed that Cassie had seemed to blossom overnight, especially tonight when she'd stripped out of that sheer gown, leaving her beautifully naked, reminding him that she was carrying his child. Reminding him how much he'd wanted her. He still did.

Brendan shook off the images for the sake of his sanity, and his dignity. He might as well come clean with Millie. She probably had maternal radar that could detect lies from miles away. "Yeah, she's pregnant."

Millie leaned over and patted his hand. "That's great, Doctor O'Connor. If anyone deserves to be a father, you do."

Brendan had serious doubts about that, but he hid

them behind another smile. "Thanks. And I'd appreciate it if you didn't say anything to anyone yet."

Millie raised one hand in an oath. "My lips are zipped, but since your wife works in the hospital, and since she's already showing, it won't take long for everyone to know."

"Yeah, that's what worries me."

"Why? Because you two just got married?" Millie blew a raspberry between her lips. "Pooh on everyone. Who cares about the timing of the nuptials? At least you did get married. Besides, when two people love each other, having a baby is only natural."

When two people love each other...

Millie's words echoed in Brendan's brain as he slowly rose from the table. He cared a great deal about Cassie, more than he'd ever cared for anyone, even Jill. But love was something he shied away from. He had loved his son but it hadn't been enough to save him. At one time he'd loved Jill, too, through the eyes of a naive kid, but he had failed her, as well, because of ambition. That emotion was too painful to acknowledge, no matter how easy Cassie would be to love. No matter how much he needed her.

Cassie needed Brendan now more than ever.

She sat on the edge of the exam table clutching the sheet to her lap in a death grip, fear spiraling through her when she noted the concern in Dr. Anderson's face. "Is something wrong?" she asked, her voice tremulous.

His careworn features softened. "I wouldn't say

DIANA PALMER

MERCENARY WOMAN

SOLDIERS OF FORTUNE

We'd like to send you **2 FREE** books and a surprise gift to introduce you to Silhouette Desire®. Accept our special offer today and

Get Ready for a totally Refreshing Experience!

HOW TO QUALIFY:

1. With a coin, carefully scratch off the silver area on the card at right to see what we have for you—2 FREE BOOKS and a FREE GIFT—ALL YOURS! ALL FREE!

2. Send back the card and you'll receive two brand-new Silhouette Desire® novels. These books have a cover price of $3.99 each in the U.S. and $4.50 each in Canada, but they are yours to keep absolutely free!

3. There's no catch. You're under no obligation to buy anything. We charge nothing—ZERO—for your first shipment and you don't have to make any minimum number of purchases—not even one!

4. The fact is, thousands of readers enjoy receiving books by mail from the Silhouette Reader Service®. They enjoy the convenience of home delivery…they like getting the best new novels at discount prices, BEFORE they're available in stores…and they love their *Heart to Heart* subscriber newsletter featuring author news, horoscopes, recipes, book reviews and much more!

5. We hope that after receiving your free books you'll want to remain a subscriber. But the choice is yours—to continue or cancel, any time at all. So why not take us up on our invitation with no risk of any kind. You'll be glad you did!

SPECIAL FREE GIFT!

We can't tell you what it is…but we're sure you'll like it! A FREE gift just for giving the Silhouette Reader Service® a try!

Visit us at www.eHarlequin.com

The **2 FREE BOOKS** we send you will be selected from **SILHOUETTE DESIRE®**, the series that brings you...highly passionate, powerful and provocative reads.

Books received may vary.

THE SILHOUETTE READER SERVICE®—Here's how it works:

Accepting your 2 free books and gift places you under no obligation to buy anything. You may keep the books and gift and return the shipping statement marked "cancel." If you do not cancel, about a month later we'll send you 6 additional books and bill you just $3.34 each in the U.S., or $3.74 each in Canada, plus 25¢ shipping & handling per book and applicable tax if any.* That's the complete price and — compared to cover prices of $3.99 each in the U.S. and $4.50 each in Canada — quite a bargain! You may cancel at any time, but if you choose to continue, every month we'll send you 6 more books, whic you may either purchase at the discount price or return to us and cancel your subscription.

*Terms and prices subject to change without notice. Sales tax applicable in N.Y. Canadian residents will be charged applicable provincial taxes and GST.

If offer card is missing write to: Silhouette Reader Service, 3010 Walden Ave., P.O. Box 1867, Buffalo NY 14240-1867

BUSINESS REPLY MAIL
FIRST-CLASS MAIL   PERMIT NO. 717-003   BUFFALO, NY

POSTAGE WILL BE PAID BY ADDRESSEE

SILHOUETTE READER SERVICE
3010 WALDEN AVE
PO BOX 1867
BUFFALO NY 14240-9952

NO POSTAGE
NECESSARY
IF MAILED
IN THE
UNITED STATES

anything's wrong. I just want to do the ultrasound to find out when this baby's due."

"You said the first of July."

He patted her arm. "According to what you've told me, that should be about right. But your uterus is much larger than it should be. I want to see if there's a reason for that."

Cassie's fear increased. "What reason?"

"Could be many things. You might be one of those women who grow pretty quickly. Or we could be dealing with a multiple birth."

Multiple birth? "You mean twins?"

He rubbed his chin. "It's been known to happen."

But how could that happen to her? What would Brendan think if that were true? And where the heck was he? She'd set the alarm as promised, but she'd already been here for almost an hour. Obviously, he'd changed his mind about coming, and he hadn't even bothered to call.

The doctor gestured to the nurse who rolled the ultrasound machine forward. He told Cassie, "Lie back so we can see what's what." After Cassie complied, he pulled up a stool to the side of the small table and pushed up Cassie's gown, exposing her belly.

He applied warmed gel to her abdomen and traced a wand over the territory for several minutes. "In a minute now you should be able to see your baby."

"Or litter," she muttered, eliciting a laugh from the doctor and nurse.

Cassie didn't find it at all funny. As much as she wanted this baby, as thrilling as it would be to have twins, she couldn't imagine what it would be like, or Brendan's reaction to the news.

But she no longer had to imagine it when Dr. Anderson proclaimed, "Congratulations, you've got a pair."

Cassie closed her eyes tightly, then opened them and turned her head toward the screen. She stared at the dark misshapen images that resembled little more than abstract masses. Tiny babies. Her babies. Hers and Brendan's.

The tears came rolling down Cassie's cheeks when the doctor pointed out the tiny pulses that indicated heartbeats. Cassie's own heart thrummed and her chest constricted with a deep maternal love. What had once been only a concept was now reality. Wonderful reality.

After the procedure was concluded, Dr. Anderson helped Cassie back up. "Questions?" he asked.

At the moment she could only think of one. "Is there anything I need to do differently now?"

"Not at this point in time. We'll watch you carefully. Just eat right, get plenty of rest. Early labor is a possibility, so I'll probably have you begin your maternity leave in your eighth month if not sooner."

"What about my activities until then?"

"As long as you're not having any problems, bleeding or contractions, you can continue with your regular routine."

"Tennis?"

"As long as you feel up to it. Exercise is good. Just don't overdo it." He grinned. "And don't take up mountain climbing, okay?"

She only had one mountain to scale, Brendan's

concern, which led to her next question. "What about lovemaking?"

"Again, it's not a problem as long as you're not having any problems. My rule of thumb is, if it makes you uncomfortable, don't do it. But as long as you don't have any pain or spotting, then you can continue as usual."

As usual. Ha! She hadn't even really gotten started yet. "Okay, then. I'll just be on my merry way."

He patted her back. "I want to see you in three weeks to check your progress. They'll give you a pamphlet about having twins on the way out. And have that husband of yours call me. Knowing Brendan, if he's like most docs, he'll have plenty of questions."

A definite understatement. She smiled tentatively. "I will." If she ever spoke to him again.

After getting dressed and making her follow-up appointment, Cassie returned to the hospital adjacent to the medical complex. She had more than enough work to keep her mind off the fact that Brendan hadn't bothered to show up. But she wasn't in the mood to confront him or go back to work just yet.

She headed past her office and down the hall to find Michelle Kempner. Right now she needed a friend. At one time that would have been Brendan, but not anymore. And that fact made her so very sad.

After rapping on the door, she heard Michelle call to her to come in. Cassie pushed into the office and closed the door behind her.

Michelle looked up from her lunch with a bright

smile. "Hey, you. I just called you a minute ago to see if you wanted anything."

Cassie glanced at Michelle's sandwich, a mound of messy cheese, meatballs and tomato sauce. Her stomach grumbled and roiled simultaneously.

Michelle dabbed at her mouth with a paper napkin and pointed at the untouched half. "You can have this if you want. I've got more than enough."

A wave of nausea washed over Cassie, forcing her into the chair across from Michelle's desk. She drew in several deep breaths until it passed. "No, thanks."

"Are you sure? You're eating for two, remember?"

"Actually, three."

Michelle stopped midbite and dropped her sandwich back onto the paper plate. "Excuse me?"

As much as Cassie valued Michelle's friendship, she had not intended to tell her about the babies before Brendan. But again she had blurted out important information without thought. "I just came back from my doctor's appointment. He did an ultrasound. I'm having twins."

Eyes bright with excitement, Michelle grinned. "That is so great! Some might say double trouble. I say twice as nice."

Under normal circumstances, Cassie would be inclined to agree. But her situation wasn't exactly normal. Yes, she had a husband to share the burden, but one who was already overly concerned about her condition. One who spent more time at the hospital than at home with her. Having twins would only raise Brendan's level of concern.

"I'm still trying to get used to the idea," Cassie said, followed by a long sigh.

"So what does the proud papa think about this?"

Cassie grabbed for a pen on the end of the desk and turned it over and over. "He doesn't know yet."

"Why?"

"Because he didn't show up at the appointment. He was supposed to be there, but I haven't seen him yet."

Michelle wiped her hands and tossed aside the napkin. "Then what are you doing here? You need to hop on the elevator and go find him."

"He's not at work. He's doing nights for a couple of weeks. As far as I know, he's home in bed, sound asleep."

"Then go home and tell him."

"I can't. I have a ton of work to do." Truth was, she couldn't tell Brendan yet for several reasons, the most important being she was still hurt that he hadn't been there for the news, not to mention her fear over his reaction.

"Work can wait for something like this, Cassie." Michelle clasped her hands in front of her. "You are planning to tell him, aren't you?"

"Of course. I just have to decide when."

"Why the ambivalence? I'd think he'd be thrilled. I know Nick would be. He'd probably announce it all over the PA system."

Cassie fought back the nip of envy. "I'm not sure how Brendan will feel about this. He's already a mother hen when it comes to my pregnancy. He's really going to freak when he finds out. He deals with multiple births every day, and with his knowledge, he's probably going to imagine every possible negative scenario.''

Michelle's expression was kind and thoughtful. ''That's part of being married to a doctor. Knowing what can happen makes it difficult for them. Nick really tries not to be too overprotective of Kelsey, but he can't help it sometimes. Just the other day he fussed at her when she rode her tricycle on the sidewalk without her helmet. You would've thought she was on a Harley in the middle of rush-hour traffic.''

Cassie's weight lifted somewhat with Michelle's logic, at least for now. ''I guess you're right. We'll both have to learn to deal with it.'' She stood. ''I need to get back to the office. I've already wasted the whole morning.''

Michelle rose and walked Cassie to the door, pausing for some parting advice. ''You know, Cassie, it's going to take some time for you both to adjust to everything. The marriage, the news about the babies. You're going to have to be patient.''

Cassie's patience was wearing thin, but she refused to give up on Brendan. ''I know. I'm trying.''

''That's all you can do.''

Feeling a sudden need to escape, to go into the solitude of her office and lick her wounds, Cassie opened the door. ''Tell Nick I said hi. I'll see you later.''

''One more thing. Is Brendan working tomorrow night?'' Michelle asked.

Cassie gripped the door. ''Probably so. Why?''

''Well, pregnant women still have to keep in shape, so I thought we could meet up tomorrow evening at the gym.''

Cassie was supposed to visit her dad, but she

could put it off for another couple of days. He'd probably never miss her. "Sounds wonderful. Is six okay?"

"Sure. I'll see you then."

Cassie headed back to her office and was immediately met by the receptionist. "Your husband called. Twice. He wants you to call him."

"Thanks."

After closing the office door behind her, Cassie picked up the phone to dial her home number. She let it ring until the answering machine kicked in, the announcement she'd recently recorded stinging her ears.

"You've reached the home of Cassie and Brendan O'Connor. We're currently occupied and can't come to the phone right now, so please leave a message. If you have a medical emergency, please contact San Antonio Memorial..."

It sounded falsely cheerful, as if she'd tried too hard to stress that they were a blissful newlywed couple. So very, very far from the truth.

She dropped the phone onto the receiver without leaving a message. Obviously Brendan was still asleep. Just as well. He might want to know about the appointment, and she didn't want to tell him about the babies over the phone. But when would she tell him? When he went back on days in two weeks? Could she really wait that long? Or would someone tell him before then?

Maybe she should go into work late tomorrow morning and catch him before he went to sleep. Maybe she should meet him for dinner tonight. She couldn't envision having that scene play out in the crowded cafeteria, and she doubted he'd want to meet her again in her office considering the botched honeymoon ploy.

She'd have to hope that he had a day off soon when they would have some quality time together beyond passing each other in the hall on their way to their respective jobs.

She needed that time with Brendan. She needed more than that from him. Patience, she reminded herself. This lack of time couldn't last forever. At least she hoped not.

Brendan heard the click of the door, apprehension gnawing at his gut. His wife was home and he could only speculate on her mood. He hoped to God that Cassie understood why he hadn't made it to the appointment. If it had been within his power to be there, he would have been. But caring for sick infants sometimes took precedence over his personal life.

Bracing for the fallout, he shifted in the chair when he heard her footsteps behind him. He wondered if it would be best to drop to his knees now and beg for forgiveness.

She looked taken aback seeing him in the kitchen, a bowl of popcorn before him and the damned cat curled up in his lap.

Her mouth dropped open for a moment before she asked, "What are you doing here?"

"I just got home."

"From work?"

Oh, hell, she didn't know he hadn't been home since last night. "Didn't you get my message?"

She tossed her briefcase onto one chair and took

the other facing him. "I tried to call. I got the machine."

"I meant the first message about me having to stay on the unit this morning."

"No, I didn't. We're training a new receptionist. Obviously she forgot."

Obviously to Brendan's detriment. "We had about three crises working at the same time. I couldn't get to the phone to let you know I wouldn't meet you at Anderson's. When I finally did get the chance to call his office, they said you'd already left."

She pushed her hair back from her face, grabbed a lone kernel of popcorn and twirled it round and round. "I thought maybe you'd overslept."

She'd thought no such thing, Brendan decided. "Maybe you thought I didn't care enough to come."

Her gaze snapped to his. "That's not true."

"Are you sure? Your mouth's twitching in the corner. It always does that when you're lying."

She dropped the popcorn and touched her fingers to the spot. "It does not!"

"Yeah, it does."

She reluctantly smiled. "Okay, so the thought did cross my mind, but only for a minute. It's the hormones. I'm feeling a little insecure lately."

Brendan figured he had done more than his share of contributing to that insecurity. "You have every reason to be doubtful, Cassie. With my schedule, I've barely given you the time of day."

Her grin deepened. "Except for last night."

God, it was great to see her smile. That and recollections of the night before, the way she had felt, tasted, woke Brendan up. All of him. And he was more than ready to take her to bed and finish what they'd started. But right now they needed to talk, at least for a while.

"Anyway," he continued, "we had one baby come down from an open heart, then another set of preterm twins."

Her eyes widened. "Twins?"

Brendan sighed. "Yeah."

"Are they okay?" she asked, her voice high, almost alarmed.

"One's fine. The other's had a few problems. I was taking care of him about the time you were seeing Anderson. Thirty-two weeks. He's underweight, but he's doing good." Brendan smiled. "His name is Montell Worthington Wilson. Big name for such a little guy."

Cassie returned his smile. "Yes, it is. And I understand why you couldn't come to the appointment. That baby needed you."

But so had Cassie, and once again Brendan had let her down. He took a drink from his soda and studied the can. "How did the appointment go?" he asked, realizing he was being selfish for not considering something so important as her first visit to the doctor. Plus, he needed to know everything was okay.

"Just some routine instructions."

Cassie's guarded tone brought Brendan's attention back to her. She'd resumed kneading the kernel, now nearly flat, and her lip twitched again, unearthing soul-wrenching fear from a fissure within Brendan that wouldn't close, no matter how many years he'd tried to seal it shut.

"What's wrong, Cassie? What did Anderson say? I swear, if something's wrong, you have to tell me."

She tossed the popcorn at him and scowled. "Oh, good grief, Brendan. He told me I'm pregnant and to take care of myself. The usual prenatal stuff."

"That's it? That's all there is?"

She smiled and took his hand from across the table. "Everything's fine. Everything's going to be okay. Would you please stop worrying?"

Feeling somewhat relieved, Brendan relaxed. "I'll try. But after dealing with what I deal with every day, you're going to have to put up with me."

"That's exactly what Michelle told me."

He didn't like the thought that Michelle Kempner was privy to his overzealous concern. But he recognized that women talked about things beyond the latest sports news. "When did you see Michelle?"

"Today after the appointment. We had lunch together."

At least Michelle would be there for Cassie when he couldn't. "So what else did you two talk about?"

"Not much. About Nick and how great he is with Kelsey. How much he enjoys being a dad."

Whether or not she intended to make Brendan feel bad, he did. "I can't blame him. It's a pretty great feeling at that."

She looked as though he'd given her a million bucks. "You think so?"

"I know so. I'm kind of looking forward to having a baby around. One that's not struggling to survive." He prayed that would be the case.

"Uh, Brendan, there's something else."

As suspected, she hadn't told him everything. He battled the apprehension. "What?"

"Well…" Her gaze slid away. "Do you have to go back in tonight?"

"Nope. I'm here until morning, barring any emergency."

Her grin crept in. "Then we're actually going to sleep in the same bed all night?" She sounded both hesitant and hopeful.

"Looks that way."

He felt a tug on the leg of his jeans, at first assuming Mister was the cause until he realized the cat was still comatose in his lap.

This time there was no mistaking Cassie's foot raising his pant leg, as well as other things. "I guess you're pretty tired having been at for work twenty-four hours," she said.

If she didn't stop with the footsies he might levitate the table. "I'm not that tired."

"So you say."

"So I know."

She slowly rose from the table, knelt and picked up her discarded shoes then sauntered toward the hall.

Brendan scooted the chair around and stared at her. "Where are you going?"

"To take a shower, then to bed."

"No late-night TV?"

Cassie's smile was coy, carefully calculated to drive him crazy. "Not tonight."

"Aren't you going to eat?"

"I had a very late lunch and I grabbed a snack on the way home. Besides, I'm not exactly hungry…for food."

The come-on look spread across her beautiful face told Brendan exactly what she was hungry for. So was he, starving like a man who'd been stranded on a womanless planet for years. He only hoped that the bologna sandwich he'd eaten would provide enough fuel to sustain the fire Cassie was creating in him.

Determined to tone down his urges for the time being, he asked one primary question. A very important question. "What did Anderson say about, uh—"

"Making love?" Cassie began unbuttoning the jacket that barely hid her swollen middle. "He said if it feels good, do it."

Brendan shifted in his chair in response to the building pressure below his belt. "Sounds like a plan."

"I believe so, too, Doctor. Care to join me in the shower?"

Boy, did he want to, but he needed to calm down. Even though he had every intention of making love to Cassie, even though she'd assured him that everything was okay with the baby, he had to take care, treat her right.

The cat gave an offending mewl of protest when Brendan set him on the ground before sliding from the chair and joining Cassie at the entrance to the hall. It took all his strength not to finish undressing her, take her to the floor where they now stood. Instead, he brushed a quick kiss over her lips and her hair back from her face.

"Tell you what," he said. "I'll meet you in bed."

"You promise you won't go anywhere else?"

He clasped her hips and pulled him against her. "Sweetheart, if I went anywhere other than to bed

in my current condition, I'd be breaking some in-
decency laws.''

She sent a pointed look at his fly then ran a slow
fingertip exactly where her gaze had been. ''Oh, I
believe you're right.''

He pulled her hand away and kissed her palm.
''Get in that shower, Cassie. Quick.''

Cassie took longer in the shower than she'd orig-
inally planned, but she wanted to draw out the tension. She wanted Brendan as worked up as she was
at the moment.

Once she was finished scrubbing from head to toe,
she toweled her hair and body, then stepped naked
from the shower. She walked to the floor-length mirror hanging on the back of the door, turned to the
left, then to the right, studying her poochy belly
from both angles, surprised at how much she had
grown in a matter of weeks. Her breasts were fuller,
heavier, and more than a little tender. Turning her
back on the mirror, she surveyed her reflection over
one shoulder. Her bottom didn't appear to be any
wider...yet. She assumed that would be changing to
accommodate the babies' birth.

She touched her tummy that now housed her precious pair. She'd hated not telling Brendan about the
babies, but after he'd talked about his day, the twin
he was caring for, she hadn't had the heart—or the
courage—to upset him more. Maybe after proving
to him that she was more than capable of making
love in her condition, she would tell him then. At
least by that time they would have taken another
step in making the marriage completely official.

On that thought, she grabbed up a towel, secured

it around her and tucked it between her breasts. Taking a deep breath, then letting out slowly, she opened the door.

The bathroom light spilled over Brendan lying on his stomach, his face turned toward her, one arm thrown over the place reserved for her. Mister had managed to curl up on the pillow above Brendan's head.

She immediately retrieved the cat with a muttered apology to Brendan and scooted the annoyed feline into the hall. Once she closed the door, she strolled to the edge of the bed and studied her husband. The limited light cast his face in shadows—his dark lashes fanned beneath his closed eyes, his mouth slack, his features relaxed. He was bare from the waist up, the rest of him covered with the sheet. She noted the rise and fall of his broad well-defined back, heard the sound of his steady breathing, and realized he was out like a light. Dead to the world. No good to her, unless she woke him.

Dropping the towel to the floor, she picked up his arm and slid into bed underneath it. Still nothing. He didn't stir or speak. He simply released an abrupt snore and turned away from her.

Frustration threatened to consume Cassie's good mood. What should she do now? Shake him awake? Scream to get his attention? Poke him in the back?

She sneaked a peek beneath the sheets. Best she could tell, he didn't have on a stitch. One well-planned touch and she might have him up and ready, raring to go.

She couldn't force herself to do it, no matter how badly she wanted to. Brendan was exhausted. He needed his sleep. Cassie needed him with a fervent desire. But what good would it do to rouse him and have him go through the motions only half-awake?

No, she would let him sleep for now. Perhaps he would wake in a few hours and make good on his promise. Maybe she would wake him if he didn't come to on his own.

Turning on her side, Cassie curled up against him and rested one arm over his hip. She buried her face between his shoulders and drew in the scent of soap, savored his heat. The man's body temperature rivaled a blast furnace.

She laid her hand against the silken mat of hair on his chest right where his strong healer's heart beat against her palm. A steady stream of emotions flowed through her, bringing with them a love so deep, so infinite, she could no longer control her tears. She couldn't hold them back any more than she could stop loving this man she held so close to her body—and her heart.

In the silence of the room she vowed to hold on to her hope that somehow, some way, he would learn to love her back.

Assured that he still slept, Cassie softly pressed her lips to his warm flesh and whispered, "I love you, Brendan O'Connor."

Seven

The shrill ring bolted Brendan upright. He automatically grabbed for the phone on the nightstand. It wasn't there.

Disoriented, he focused on the other side of the bed where a figure lay curled up in a cocoon of covers. Awareness came back to him slowly.

He rested his arms on bent knees, lowered his head, and delivered a litany of curses directed at his demanding schedule, his stupidity. He recalled the sound of running water from the adjacent bathroom while he had waited for Cassie to come to him. He remembered feeling euphoric, almost relaxed had it not been for the dire need to make love to Cassie. Obviously he'd been so relaxed he'd fallen asleep.

The phone chimed again. Reaching over Cassie, he plucked the cordless from the charger and answered with an ill-tempered, "Speak."

"Aren't we the jolly old fellow this morning."
Millie's raspy tone grated on Brendan's already-raw
nerves.

He cleared the hitch from his throat. "What time
is it?"

"Time for you to get down here. Albers needs
you to attend a preterm delivery. All hell's breaking
loose on the unit."

Brendan glanced at the clock—4 a.m. He'd been
asleep for six hours but he felt as though it had only
been twenty minutes.

Cassie stirred beside him, turned onto her back,
then stretched her arms above her head. The sheet
fell slightly to one side, revealing the curve of her
bare breast illuminated by the faint light spilling in
from the window. The tempting sight had Brendan's
body making immediate demands and his brain calling up another few choice oaths directed at the hospital.

"Can't someone else do it, Millie?" He had other
things he needed to do. Wanted to do. Namely, en-
gage in some predawn lovemaking.

"According to Dr. Albers, you've got about
twenty minutes tops to get here or you'll miss the
delivery and encounter the head honcho's wrath."

Brendan tapped his forehead against his bent
knees. "You guys are about to do me in."

"Don't blame me, Dr. O'Connor. I'm just the
messenger."

"Okay. I'll be there ASAP." He clicked off the
phone without giving Millie a chance to respond and
tossed it on the end of the bed.

He glanced at Cassie again, then pulled his gaze
away. How long had she been there, curled up be-

side him? How in God's name could he have passed out, knowing she was about to join him in bed to finally satisfy that need? And why hadn't she punched him awake? Maybe she *had* tried. Or maybe she'd changed her mind.

"I take it you have to go in." Cassie's tone was husky with sleep and disappointment.

He shot another look her way once more, but only for a moment, otherwise his position at the hospital might be in peril. "Yeah, unfortunately I do."

Cassie snapped on the bedside lamp, drawing his attention back to her. Without regard for her nudity, or Brendan's current condition, she propped up against the headboard. Her blond hair was tangled and incredibly sexy. Her breasts were full, unencumbered, a welcome sight for tired eyes. A sight that would be the death of his job if he didn't get away from her now.

Before he could move, Cassie ran her delicate fingertips down his forearm. "How long do you have?"

About thirty seconds if she kept that up. "Not much longer if I want to get there on time."

She stroked his arm back and forth in a slow torturous tempo, calling up images in Brendan's mind of her stroking other places. "Do you *have* to be there on time?"

"If I don't want to get fired, I do."

She turned on her side to face him, brushed the sheet aside, and revealed everything to his eyes— the curve of her waist, the flair of her hip, the light shading at the juncture of her thighs. "Are you sure you don't have a few more minutes?"

Brendan was only sure about one thing. He was

about to lose it, and he couldn't do a damn thing to stop it.

He fell back with a groan and wrapped her in his arms. Their bodies touched in all the right places. She was soft and warm and smelled like flowers. He was rock hard and ready and primed to disregard his responsibility. The kiss they shared turned fiery, desperate. Brendan clasped her bottom and tugged her against him. Cassie circled her arms around him and draped her leg over his hip. They were so close that only one thing could bring them closer. He touched her warm, wet heat until he had her gasping and clawing his back. Brendan balanced on the brink of giving everything up to the moment. The sound of the phone hitting the floor forced him back into reality.

He reluctantly let her go and sat at the edge of the bed, streaking both hands over his face.

"Brendan." His name left her lips on a slow moan.

"I'm sorry. I have to go." Seemed all he'd done lately was apologize to her. He imagined she was as tired of hearing "I'm sorry" as he was as tired of having reasons to say it. He planned to put an end to any need for apologies this evening, even if it meant calling in sick. In a way he was sick—sick and tired of interruptions.

Brendan stood and headed toward the bathroom. Before he opened the door, he faced her again, thankful to see that she had covered herself. "I'm going to trade off with one of the other docs and work the rest of the day. I swear I'll be home tonight, all night. We're going to finish this, even if I have to cut the phone lines."

Eyes wide with delight, she smiled. "Promise?"

"Promise." He paused with a hand on the knob. "By the way, why didn't you wake me last night?"

She shrugged. "I think I could've dropped a grenade in the bed and you wouldn't have moved."

"You should've tried harder to get me up."

"I did this morning, and quite successfully." Her grin deepened as she shot a glance at the source of his current discomfort.

He looked down then smiled back at her. "Yeah, but don't worry. I don't think any part of me will be going to sleep anytime soon."

"I hope not."

"I guarantee it. And you better be ready, Cassie O'Connor."

Her face lit up with out-and-out joy. Brendan was amazed that something so simple as using the name they now shared would so obviously please her. He was even more amazed that the acknowledgment of her status as his wife had come so easily. And tonight he would show her exactly how much that was beginning to mean to him.

As it turned out, Brendan could have made love to Cassie and still had almost an hour to spare.

Preterm, in this instance, meant thirty-six weeks. The baby took his own sweet time being born and weighed in at seven pounds. No telling how much the boy would have weighed had he waited another four weeks to make an appearance. Lucky for the mother he wasn't any larger, Brendan decided, since she wasn't much bigger than Cassie.

Cassie.

She was all he thought about while examining the

infant who bellowed in protest and appeared to be healthy as a horse. Even though the early labor didn't hold all that much risk, in Brendan's logical mind he understood the need to err on the side of caution. For that reason he didn't resent coming in for the birth, or the fact this particular baby was in great shape—a valued change from the usual circumstances Brendan dealt with daily. But Brendan did harbor a little resentment that someone else on the unit couldn't have attended this particular birth so he could attend to his wife.

But come famine or flood, Brendan was determined to finish out the shift and go home to finish what he had begun this morning. What they had begun two nights ago in Cassie's office. What she had begun that first night she'd kissed him months ago.

Once the baby was transferred to the regular nursery, Brendan stopped Dr. Anderson who had delivered the baby boy. "You got a minute, Jim?"

The OB smiled although his face looked haggard. "What's on your mind?"

Brendan had several questions he needed answered about Cassie's pregnancy, but the man appeared as though he was about to drop on the spot. "Never mind. I'll call you later. Looks like you've had a rough night."

"You could say that. Three deliveries since six p.m. I'm getting too old for this routine. I'm thinking about hanging it up this spring, at least the deliveries."

"You can't do that yet. You still have to deliver mine."

He pushed his glasses up on the bridge of his

nose. "You can bet I wouldn't miss that, Brendan. It's not every day you get to bring a set of twins into the world."

Obviously, the doctor had Cassie mixed up with someone else, Brendan thought. "Far as I know, Jim, we're only having one."

A blanket of confusion spread over Anderson's face. "Cassie didn't tell you?"

Brendan felt as though a five-ton meteor had landed in the middle of his chest. "Tell me what?"

Anderson raked the blue paper cap off his head and studied the floor. "Sorry, Brendan. I didn't re-alize you didn't know about the babies yet."

Brendan had a hard time pulling his voice out from under the shock. "Babies?"

"Yeah. Two. I confirmed that through ultrasound during her appointment yesterday."

Betrayal had Brendan in a choke hold, threatening to suffocate him. But he grabbed for an excuse to hand the discomfited doctor. "I've been on almost two days straight. I'm sure she was planning some special way to tell me tonight." Or maybe she hadn't planned to tell him at all. That thought brought on a good dose of anger.

Anderson looked somewhat relieved. "That's probably right. Anyway, if everything goes well, which I have no reason to believe it won't, the ba-bies will be fine."

"I hope so."

Patting him on the back, Anderson said, "Try not to worry too much, Brendan. You and I both know that most multiples, especially twins, end up fine. Besides, you're still on your honeymoon. Enjoy your wife's company. When those babies get here,

you're not going to have a lot of quality time together.''

"Yeah, you're right. But I don't want to do anything that might compromise the pregnancy."

"You won't hurt anything by making love, if
that's what's worrying you." Anderson let go a jolly
laugh. "Enjoy that, too, while you still can. This
business tends to make us old men before our time."

At the moment, Brendan felt ancient, much older
than his thirty-three years. "Thanks. Guess I'll let
you get back to work now. I need to get back, too."
He needed to escape and digest the unexpected
news.

After a quick goodbye, Brendan strode down the
hall, anger dogging his every step. The past kept
repeating itself, at least where the women in his life
were concerned. Jill hadn't told him she was pregnant, now Cassie hadn't bothered to tell him about
the twins.

More determined than ever to have the night off,
Brendan bypassed the unit and headed toward Albers's office to make his demands. He had to get
home at a decent time. Get home to Cassie who had
a hell of a lot of explaining to do.

Cassie had expected the feelings of exhilaration
after her workout with Michelle. She hadn't expected to see Brendan's car parked in the driveway.

She'd already showered before leaving the gym
in hopes of having at least thirty minutes to prepare
for Brendan's return. She wanted to fix a special
meal, put on some makeup, dress in something sexy.
That wasn't to be since Brendan had obviously gotten off earlier than expected. Maybe he was as anx-

ious to see her as she was to see him. Maybe dinner could consist of pizza and while they waited for the delivery guy, they could have dessert first.

Cassie found the door unlocked and Brendan sitting in the recliner, one hand wrapped around a beer, his face molded into a stern mask. Must have been a bad day, Cassie decided. Not a problem. She planned to make him forget his troubles in some very creative ways.

After dropping her bag onto the sofa, Cassie pushed her damp hair from her face and smiled. "Hey, I didn't expect to see you for at least another hour."

Brendan sat, stoic as a redwood, no welcoming smile to greet her. He gave her a quick once-over, glanced at her gym bag, then centered his solemn gaze back on her face. "Where have you been?" His tone was void of friendliness, bordering on fury.

Surely he wasn't going to make an issue out of the exercise. If so, she would dispel all of his concerns, or at least try. "I've been at the gym with Michelle. I met her for a quick workout. Dr. Anderson said exercise is good for me."

He leaned forward and dangled the beer between his parted legs. "You didn't tell me you were going."

"I didn't think it mattered. Besides, I thought I would be home before you."

"What else haven't you told me, Cassie?"

Here it comes. "Oh, please, Brendan. I jogged on the treadmill for a while, swam a few laps. I didn't overdo it."

"I talked to Anderson today."

Cassie's breath hitched and she tried to smile, look innocent. "What about?"

"You know what about. You lied to me."

He knew about the twins. Fear and regret bubbled up inside Cassie. Her knees felt too frail to hold her weight so she braced one hand on the back of the sofa. "Brendan, I haven't lied. I just—"

"Didn't bother to tell me? When did you plan to do that? When they were born?"

She'd never seen Brendan so angry. The intense fire in his eyes, the ire in his tone, alarmed her. Why, oh, why had she waited to tell him? Her delay was going to ruin their night, maybe ruin everything.

Cassie took a few guarded steps forward. "I planned to tell you last night, in bed, but you fell asleep."

He meticulously set the beer bottle on the end table then regarded her for what seemed like an eternity, his features taut, no less angry. "You should've told me the minute you found out."

"How was I supposed to do that, Brendan? You didn't come to the appointment."

"You should have called me."

"How? You didn't even bother to have someone call to tell me where you were. It's the least you could have done."

"I was working, dammit. Making a living."

"Taking care of everyone who needs you. Everyone but me."

He bolted out of the chair, his hands fisted at his sides. "That's not fair, Cassie. It's what I do. I don't have a choice."

"You have plenty of choices. You're afraid to make them. You're afraid to have someone need you other than your patients because you're worried you might need someone in return. And that scares the hell out of you, doesn't it?''

Some unidentified emotion passed over his expression. Maybe guilt. Maybe awareness. Cassie didn't know which, but at the moment she didn't care. She only cared about making him understand.

"Put yourself in my place, Brendan. After what you've told me the past few months about your concern for your patients, and the way you've treated me since you found out I was pregnant, I didn't know how to tell you without worrying you more.''

"I'm not that weak. I could've handled the news.''

She took a chance and moved closer to him. "Could you? You're not handling it all that well now.''

He stepped back, away from her. He might as well have punched her in the jaw. "You made me promise we would always be honest with each other, Cassie.''

"I'm trying, but you're not. Something is going on with you, Brendan. Something you've buried so deep you won't let anyone see it. I want to know what drives you to give all of yourself to your patients. What makes you so afraid of getting close to anyone else?''

"Maybe there's nothing left.''

"I don't want to believe that.''

"Well, I tell you what I want. I want—'' His gaze slipped away as he rubbed a hand over his jaw.

"What do you want, Brendan?''

"I don't know anymore.''

Cassie hugged her arms close against her breasts

in an attempt to block out the pain in her heart. "I tell you one thing that's apparent. You don't want me."

Needing to escape, Cassie headed down the hallway and pushed into the bedroom. She toed out of her sneakers, opened the closet and chucked them inside. Pausing, she surveyed the row of Brendan's clothes lined up across from hers. To anyone else, the scene would serve as a testament to an average couple cohabitating like any other. But it was only a pretense, exactly the way this marriage was turning out to be.

"I'm sorry, Cassie."

Cassie was startled by the sound of Brendan's sudden apology, even more surprised by his arms circling her from behind to hold her close. He brought his lips to her ear and said, "You're right. I don't blame you for not telling me." He brushed a kiss across her cheek. "But you're wrong about one thing. I do want you."

He rimmed her ear with the tip of his tongue; his warm breath danced down her neck. "No matter where I am, or what time of day, all I think about is making love to you, being inside you again. It's driving me crazy."

He lulled her with his sensual words, with his strong arms surrounding her like a soft blanket during winter's chill. But still she battled her concerns, reluctant to give in unless she knew this wasn't only desire speaking. Others had wanted her before Brendan, solely from a physical perspective. She had made a mistake believing that by giving in to intimacy, she might cultivate love. It hadn't happened.

Admittedly, she wanted Brendan in every way.

She also wanted more. She wanted everything, including his heart, his love.

Cassie sighed. "Making love won't make everything right between us, Brendan."

"I know, but it's a start."

Cassie wanted desperately to believe that might be true, that it could be a start. That connecting through lovemaking would create a deeper emotional union. It certainly would for her, but what about Brendan? Should she take the risk only to be disappointed later?

Brendan stroked his knuckles down her cheek. "Can we forget about everything tonight? Can we just *be* together?"

Such a tempting thought, Cassie decided. Then his fingertips grazed her breasts and he pulled her closer. She couldn't resist him, couldn't resist taking one more chance—*if* he gave up the crazy notion that she was fragile. "Only if you'll treat me like a lover and not just the mother of your children."

"I want you to be my lover. I need you, Cassie. So bad I hurt."

"Then prove it."

Turning her around, he clasped her hand and slid her palm slowly, slowly down his chest, his abdomen and lower until it came to rest against the swell beneath his fly. "Is that proof enough?"

Cassie brushed her thumb back and forth over the crest, delighted when Brendan's control began to falter, confirmed by the way his eyes grew shuttered and his lips parted. She stepped back and closed the closet door, then leaned against it for support. "That's pretty strong evidence, Doctor. Now what do you plan to do with it?"

Eyes darkened by desire, Brendan spanned the
small space between them, tracking his zipper down
as he went. Cassie thought he might actually take
her right there but he didn't. He did work her sweatshirt up and over her head then turned her toward
the door. After he unsnapped her bra, she shrugged
it off but before she could face him again, he
stopped her by moving her damp hair aside to ply
gentle kisses between her shoulder blades, bending
to continue down the column of her spine until he
reached her waistband. He slid the sweats and panties down her hips and worked them off her trembling legs.

Straightening again, he turned her into his arms
and delivered a deep, slow-burn kiss. A kiss so complete, so full of need, it captured Cassie's concerns
and pitched them away.

Brendan broke the kiss and took her hand. He led
her to the bed, placed her on the edge, then began
to undress while she watched. He tugged his ragged
T-shirt over his head, bringing his sculpted chest
into view, a silken tangle of dark hair centered between his pale-brown nipples. She followed the path
his hands took as he skimmed out of his jeans, then
his briefs. His hips were narrow, his thighs lean and
well-defined beneath the covering of masculine hair.
And above that, absolute verification that he did
want her completely.

Not allowing her much time to appreciate the
sight, Brendan went to his knees before her. He nuz-
zled her neck, kissed her jaw then worked his way
down to her breasts. He played her with his mouth,
graced her nipples with soft strokes of his tongue
until her body wept for him.

Brendan straightened and offered her a sensual smile. "Is this what you had in mind, Cassandra?"

She answered with little more than a nod and a small sound.

He then lowered his head to trace his tongue over her bare thighs as her breath stilled with anticipation. He rested his lips on the swell of her belly for a long moment. Just when Cassie thought he was about to reconsider, he murmured, "Lie back."

When she answered his low command, he pulled her hips closer to the edge and nudged her trembling legs apart, awakened her senses with his intimate kiss, worshipped her with his gentle lips, finessed her flesh with his tongue.

No matter how hard she tried to hold back the surge, the climax came too soon beneath Brendan's bold exploration. She shook uncontrollably and clutched the comforter.

Then he was there, rolling her into his strong arms and holding her close to his side. He positioned them face-to-face, raised her leg over his hip and entered her with a slow glide.

They sighed in harmony, moved in sync, clung to each other as they caught a steady cadence. He treated her with such care, with such aching tenderness that Cassie fought tears of sheer joy and undeniable love.

She had never felt so appreciated before, so close to being home, to being someone that mattered to someone else—the man she loved with every part of her being.

Brendan continued to touch her gently, arousing sensations she didn't know existed, traveling right to the carnal core of her. The pressure began to build and build once again when he whispered his praise with enthralling, sensual words. She wanted him closer, in her arms, against her pounding heart.

Pulling him over, she stared up into his eyes now full of concern.

"Cassie, I'm too heavy."

She placed a fingertip against his lips to silence his protest. "I want to be closer Brendan. I want to feel every part of you. You're not going to hurt me, I promise."

Cassie wrapped her legs around his waist and in turn unleashed something in Brendan, something wild and welcome and, oh, so incredible. His thrusts grew more demanding, his touch more insistent, his sudden kiss all consuming.

The wave broke then, washing Cassie in liquid fire. Brendan followed soon after, whispering her name as he climaxed with a shudder.

With Brendan still securely in her arms, she closed her eyes and let the tears fall, creating a damp path to where Brendan's cheek met hers.

He raised his face, more worry in his eyes. "I hurt you, didn't I?"

She sent him a shaky smile. "On the contrary, I've never felt so well in my life." So well loved.

As if he didn't quite believe her, he slipped from her body, turned them to face each other and enfolded her against his chest. "I'd never forgive myself if I did anything to hurt you or the babies."

"You didn't, so stop worrying. I'm just feeling a little emotional, that's all."

He kissed her forehead. "Not surprising. You're getting a double dose of hormones."

He had no idea that her sudden emotional outburst

had nothing to do with hormones, and everything to do with her love for him.

Cassie's heart felt weighted with that knowledge. She wondered what he would do if she told him, if she came right out and said how she felt. But before she could make the revelation, Brendan spoke first.

"There's something I have to tell you, Cassie."

Her heart welled with hope, but it died when she raised her head and noted his tightly clenched jaw. "What is it?"

A long, ragged sigh drifted from his lips.

"His name was Blake William O'Connor."

Eight

Brendan struggled against the sudden pain, the need to retreat from the memories. But he couldn't hide from it any longer. It wouldn't be fair. Cassie deserved to know everything.

Not here, he thought. Not in bed with her so close. It would be all too easy to forget by making love to her again instead of facing his past. He couldn't do that. She needed to know the truth.

Slipping his arm from beneath her, he left the bed before he changed his mind.

"Where are you going?" she asked.

"I need something to drink." He pulled her robe from the hook on the bathroom door and offered it to her. "Put this on and come with me."

He slipped on his jeans; she slipped on her robe and followed him into the kitchen. He opted for instant coffee, strong and black, which Cassie declined, then seated himself across from her at the small table. He wrapped his hands around the mug, trying to absorb some of the warmth. It didn't help. Right now he felt cold to the marrow, chilled by the memories he didn't want to resurrect but knew he must.

Cassie sat with arms folded beneath her breasts, looking at him expectantly.

Brendan wasn't sure where to begin, how to tell her. He mustered all his courage and prepared to spill his guts. "It was thirteen years ago. I thought I was over it. But when I almost lost the Neely baby, I realized it wasn't over at all. That night I went to your place, it was the anniversary of my son's death. He died when he was only a few hours old."

She sighed. "Oh, Brendan, I wish you'd told me."

"I wasn't ready then. I'm not really ready now, but it's past time for you to know."

She laid a gentle touch on his arm. "Just take your time."

He had all the time in the world, and too much to say. "I didn't even know about him until after he was born."

"Why not?"

Brendan took a long drink of coffee, still needing more warmth but not finding any. "His mother was my high school girlfriend. We split up when I was in my second year of premed. The night I told her it was over, Jill was pretty desperate, and I gave in. One huge mistake. We didn't use any protection, like a couple of fools."

"You were kids, Brendan. But I understand how

you must have felt, not knowing about your baby. Did she ever tell you her reasons?''

''Probably the same reasons you didn't tell me about the twins. I can be one self-absorbed bastard, Cassie.''

''You're wrong, Brendan. You're committed to your work, your patients. There's nothing wrong with that.''

He glanced at her with disbelief. ''Considering what I've put you through, I don't see how you can say that. Even back then, my career was foremost on my mind. School, making the grade. Only now it's my work on the unit. Nothing's changed.''

''A lot has changed. You're an adult now.''

He released a humorless laugh. ''So what's my excuse? I keep making the same mistakes. I can't stop this drive I have to save those babies, though God knows I can't always do that. But it's so damned important to me that I do.''

Cassie paused for a moment, then searched his eyes. ''Maybe it's because you've never really grieved for your child, and every sick infant becomes him in a way. You've gone through some of the motions of grieving, but you haven't really accepted his death. What happened with Monica Neely, the anniversary, served as a trigger. And now that I'm pregnant, it's only added fuel to the fire.''

''I understand that on some level. But it doesn't make it any easier.''

''I know it doesn't.'' She looked away then brought her dark, compassionate eyes back to him. ''Did you see him?''

He wasn't sure he wanted to get into that, but the bittersweet memories returned regardless of his indecision. "Yeah, I saw him. He was born in Jill's seventh month, weighed all of two pounds. Jill called my parents and told them, and they called me. I got there as soon as I could, a few hours after he was born."

Brendan opened and closed his fist, remembering. "It was strange. He looked perfect, perfect hands, feet. But he was so damned small. They wouldn't let me hold him."

"Why?"

"He was too sick. And Jill's parents didn't want me there. They blamed me. They were probably right to blame me."

"No, they weren't," Cassie said adamantly. "You didn't know."

In his rational mind, Brendan recognized that was true. He also knew that he hadn't bothered to contact Jill, at the very least see how she was doing. Maybe then she would have told him she was pregnant. Maybe not.

"It doesn't matter now, Cassie. It's done. I can't change anything. I only wish..."

She touched his hand. "You wish what?"

Brendan's throat tightened from the threatening sadness. "I only wish I'd been there when he was born. Before he was born. Jill didn't have any pre-natal care."

"And you think you're responsible for that?"

"Yeah. I should have stayed in touch with her. Said I'm sorry for everything."

"Did you—" Cassie paused for a long moment "—did you love her?"

"I thought I did at one time. But once I was on

my own, I realized it was more teenage lust than love. That's what got us into trouble.''

Cassie slipped a napkin from the holder on the table and folded it back and forth. "That's why you were so hard on the Kinsey couple."

"Yeah. It's pretty tough watching kids make the same mistakes that I did. Sometimes I wish I could go back, do things over, but I know I can't."

"No, you can't. What's done is done." She looked at him with a remarkably calm demeanor. Brendan recognized she was now in the counselor mode.

Brendan sighed, pelted by more memories. "It's pretty damned ironic. I was there when he took his final breath, but I wasn't there when he took his first, and I've had to live with that for thirteen years."

Cassie took both his hands into hers and brought them to her lips. He looked up to see tears welling in her eyes. "I'm so sorry, Brendan. But I'm glad you told me."

"Maybe this was a bad idea. Now I've upset you."

"Of course I'm upset. If it upsets you, it's going to upset me."

"It's not your problem, Cassie. It's mine."

She released his hands and sat back. "But it affects our relationship. It's affected everything you do, why you chose your career, why you're so afraid of something happening to our babies. But you're going to have to let go of it."

He damned sure wished he could. But he wouldn't be able to until his children were born healthy. "I'm trying, but you have to understand.

You're in a high-risk situation. Anything could go wrong with the pregnancy.''

"Couldn't everything go right?"

Brendan stared into his half-full cup, feeling completely empty. "Yeah, that's possible. It's probably likely. But I can't help but worry over the outcome. Maybe having twins is my punishment."

"Punishment?" Her voice rose with anger; hurt sparked in her dark eyes. "I'm so sorry that you think of our babies as *punishment*."

God, he hated that he couldn't seem to control his stupid mouth. "I didn't mean that the way it sounded."

Cassie yanked back the chair and stood with her hands clenched tightly at her sides. "Let's get one thing straight. I didn't trap you, Brendan, like your teenage girlfriend. I didn't mean for this to happen, but it has, and I'm glad it did. I love these babies with all my heart and I realize that our children will never replace your son. But no matter how many infants you save, you can't bring him back."

"I realize that, dammit."

"Do you know what I realize? I'm just as guilty as you are, hanging on to the past. I lived with a father who blamed me for his wife's departure. I have tried all my life to please him, to prove to him that I'm worthy of his love. And you know what? I'm tired of trying to convince the men in my life that I have needs, too."

Brendan mentally flinched over the comparison to her father, a man who obviously failed to give Cassie what she needed when she was growing up, exactly what Brendan was doing—failing to give her what she needed now.

Cassie laid a protective hand on her abdomen. "I don't see this pregnancy as some kind of punishment, Brendan. I see it as a gift, and I only hope that someday you'll see that, too, regardless of what happens with us."

With that, she spun around and headed toward the bedroom, leaving Brendan alone with his remorse.

For God's sake, she was his wife. Tonight she had become that in every sense of the word, but in turn he had lost his best friend.

Resting his face in his hands, Brendan fought the rising tide of emotion, the penetrating loss, the tears he had never cried for his child. But he didn't let them come, afraid if he did, he might never stop.

Cassie couldn't seem to stop thinking about Brendan's revelations, even though she had more than enough work to keep her occupied. Her sadness came on many levels. She mourned the loss of his child, mourned for the wonderful man who lived in a prison of his own making, mourned the dwindling hope that their marriage might survive.

He hadn't come back to bed last night. That morning she had found him asleep on the sofa and had decided not to wake him. She didn't want his apologies; she wanted him to make a commitment to their marriage. And she was beginning to realize that might not ever happen.

Cassie had vowed to never give up on him, but how could that be possible if he had all but given up on himself? Didn't he know how valued he was at the hospital? How much she valued him? Couldn't he see how much she loved him?

She had come so close to telling him, and now

she wished she had. Not that it would change anything. No matter how much she loved him, Brendan had to heal himself. She didn't want to throw in the towel, but she didn't have the desire to remain absent from his heart, just like she had been invisible to her father in her formative years. She also couldn't stand the thought of being without him, but it seemed as though that might be her only recourse. Maybe if she wasn't accessible, then he might come to realize that what they had together would be worth fighting for. Maybe then he would miss her enough to want her back. Or maybe not.

Despite her determination to force Brendan's hand, Cassie snatched up the phone after the first ring, hoping it was him.

"Mrs. O'Connor?"

She couldn't deny her disappointment when she heard the woman's voice. "Yes?"

"This is Nancy from the ER. They've brought your father in, possible MI."

A heart attack. Cassie gripped the phone and fought the sudden wave of nausea. "Is it bad?"

"We don't know yet. We're going to run some tests to determine the extent of the damage to his heart. Dr. Granger's with him now."

"I'm on my way."

Cassie raced out the door and headed to the emergency room. If ever she needed Brendan, it would be now. But she wouldn't call him. She would deal with her dad on her own. She would deal with Brendan later.

Brendan handed the chart to Millie and rolled his shoulders against the mounting tension and spring-tight muscles, concerned over one tiny patient's blood oxygen levels. "What are baby Rosenfield's sats?"

"She's at eighty-nine."

"Get a blood gas. They're bringing the new admit down. Be sure they've drawn a hematacrit, the mother's diabetic. And tell Albers I'm taking a break or I won't be any good to anyone."

Millie gave Brendan a salute as he left for the break room. He had to call Cassie, see if she was okay. See if she was still speaking to him after last night. He'd gone into work at noon and had almost stopped by her office. Almost. He'd seen no need in upsetting her further while she was trying to work. At least he could gage her attitude over the phone, and then maybe she would agree to hang around awhile until he went on dinner break. They had a lot to discuss, and he had his work cut out for him if he wanted to make amends.

Slipping into the break room, Brendan picked up the wall phone and dialed her extension. Unsuccessful, he had the operator reroute him to the social services receptionist.

"I need to leave a message for Cassie O'Connor."

"She won't be back in this afternoon."

Brendan checked his watch. Barely 5 p.m. Cassie rarely left the office before six. "She's already gone home?"

"No."

He clenched his jaw tight to stifle a curse. Getting information out of this woman was like pulling a stubborn splinter. "Look, this is her husband. Did she say where she was going?"

"Oh, Dr. O'Connor," she said, sounding if she'd suddenly awakened to a new world. "You didn't know? Cassie's in the ER. She's—"

Brendan slammed the phone down, sprinted up the hall and shoved into the elevator right before the doors closed. He pounded the first-floor button, panic gnawing at his gut. Something was wrong with Cassie, and he couldn't help but think this was his fault. Again.

He bore down on the ER desk, taking the nurse by surprise, a big burly guy who looked like he could eat nails over the interruption. "Is my wife here?"

He gave him a quick once-over. "Who are you?"

"Dr. O'Connor. My wife is Cassandra. Cassandra O'Connor."

He rolled back the chair and looked over his shoulder. "I don't have an O'Connor listed on the board."

"She's pregnant. Maybe she's been sent to the OB floor."

"We haven't had an OB admit, and I've been on since three."

None of this made any sense. "She's a social worker here. Her office said she's in the ER, so look again."

The guy rolled a pencil between his beefy fingers. "Okay, I remember now. She should be up on six, at the cath lab. They brought her father in, Coy Allen."

Brendan breathed a sigh of relief. "Thanks."

He turned around and headed for the elevator once again. Although his concern for Cassie had subsided somewhat now that he knew she was okay, he still worried that the stress of her father's illness could affect her, as well.

Why in the hell hadn't she called him? He knew the answer to that. She probably didn't want him around. Too bad. He intended to make her see that he was going to be there for her whether she wanted him to or not.

Once he reached the cardiology floor's waiting room, he scanned the area and found Cassie talking to Jared Granger.

He strode to them and blurted out, "What's happening?"

Cassie looked startled. "How did you know I was here?"

"I managed to find out after several minor roadblocks." He turned his attention to Jared and held out his hand. "Are you taking care of Cassie's dad?"

Jared shook his hand. "Yeah. He's had a mild MI. Right now he's stable. I was just telling Cassie that I want to go ahead and do a bypass. He's got some hefty blockage in four arteries. I want to get that taken care of before he infarcts again."

"Are you going to do it tonight?"

"Yeah. I'm about to scrub in. They'll have him prepped and ready to go soon."

"Can I see him first?" Cassie asked.

"He's pretty out of it right now, but you can go in for a few minutes," Jared said.

"I won't take long. I just need to see him in case..." Her gaze slipped away along with her words.

Jared patted her arm while Brendan looked on, wanting desperately to hold her, take her in his arms, tell her it would be okay. But it wasn't okay. She looked tired, distressed, and more than a little irritated over Brendan's sudden arrival.

"There is a risk to any surgery, Cassie," Jared said. "But if all goes well, he should do fine. I'll send someone out and let you know how it's going. Hang in there." After shaking Brendan's hand again, he left.

Cassie's rigid frame, her tense expression, her weary eyes, indicated to Brendan that this whole mess was taking a toll on her, physically and emotionally.

"Why don't you sit down for a minute?" he said.

She nailed him with a dark, serious stare. "I'm fine, Brendan. You can go back to work now."

He should get back; the staff was awaiting his direction on several patients. No one had a clue where he was. But he couldn't leave Cassie until he knew everything was okay, that she was okay. "This surgery's going to take several hours. Why don't you go home for a while and rest? I'll keep in touch with the OR."

"I'm not going anywhere. I'm not leaving him until the surgery is over."

"That could be past midnight. I doubt you got much sleep last night. You need to rest."

"I need to see my dad. I have to talk to him."

Brendan couldn't get a hold on his frustration. "You need to take care of yourself first, Cassie. He probably won't even remember you being there."

"It doesn't matter. I'm doing this for me as much as I am for him."

"Why? Do you think what you say is going to make any difference in the way he treats you?"

"Maybe not, but I'll feel better. I want him to know that despite all the garbage between us, I still love him."

"And you think that if you love him enough, he might eventually love you back?"

She braced one hand on the back of a chair, her features even more somber than before. "As a matter of fact, I don't think that at all. I know that's not reality. I've also realized that no matter how much I love you, Brendan, and I do love you, that you're not going to love me back, either. That's why I've come to a decision about this marriage."

Brendan felt as though he'd been knifed in the gut. "What decision?"

"I want you to move out. I know you don't want to be with me and I don't want you to feel I'm holding you there. You're free to go. I won't stop you from seeing the babies, but I can't live like we've been living anymore."

"But—"

"There's nothing more to say. I have to see my father now." With that she turned away from him and headed down the corridor.

Shock held Brendan in place, both from her declaration of love and her insistence that he get out of her life. But what could he expect? He had dealt her nothing but grief. She deserved better. He sure as hell didn't deserve her love. But the thought of leaving her constricted his chest with remorse.

Collapsing into a chair, he closed his eyes and tried to erase Cassie's image from his mind. Instead, he recalled the times they had shared as good friends, and recently as lovers. God, he didn't want her to love him. He didn't deserve that kind of commitment. But he couldn't imagine not having her in his life even though he had probably destroyed what little faith she had in him. Not surprising since he had so little belief that he could ever be the man she needed.

Still, he had to convince her that he didn't want to live without her. Somehow he would have to find a way to tell her what was in his heart, if she chose to give him another chance.

"Dad?"

Cassie gently shook her father's arm as he lay on the small hospital bed, his skin ruddy and his features slack. He was so still, looked so helpless, very unlike the headstrong man she had known growing up.

His eyes drifted open, and his brows narrowed as he tried to focus on her face. "Cassie?"

"Yes, it's me. How are you feeling?"

"Like I've been plowed over by a big rig."

He tried to sit up but she stopped him with a hand on his shoulder. "Be still. They're about to take you up for surgery."

Amazingly, he smiled. "Must be bad for you to be hanging around here playing nursemaid to your old man."

"I was at work when they called me. I talked to your doctor. He said everything's going to be okay."

Apprehension passed over his expression. "Could be, but I'm not laying money on that."

"You have to think positively. Concentrate on getting well."

"I might not."

"Don't say that."

"You think what you will."

"I think you need to stop being so stubborn."

He barked out a laugh. "A little late for me to be changin' that." He drew in a broken breath then exhaled slowly. "Before I have this operation, there's something I'm gonna tell you."

Cassie braced for a lecture, determined to keep her temper in check. "You don't have to talk now. You need to rest."

"Dammit, little girl, I'm gonna say this, and you're gonna listen. I *have* to say it in case I don't make it."

"Okay, Daddy, don't get yourself all worked up."

He frowned. "What did you say?"

"Don't get upset."

"I mean what you called me. Daddy. Do you know the last time you said that?"

Cassie shook her head. As long as she could remember, he had always been simply "Dad."

His eyes drifted shut then opened slowly. "I'm thinking you were about eight. I bought you that pink bike you bugged me about, the one with the streamers hanging from the handlebars. Took me all Christmas Eve to put it together. When you saw it, you stuck up that chin of yours and told me you were going to race every boy on the block and win."

Cassie smiled with remembrance. "I do remember that."

"I tell you, you were independent as all get-out. Even as a baby. I had to walk the floor with you at night cause you got it in your head you liked the late shows. I don't think you slept all night till you were almost two. Your aunt Vida said you did most of your sleeping during the day so you could be up with the old man when he got home. Crazy woman.''

A strong realization began to move through Cassie's mind, the realization that her father had once cared about her and exactly what he had gone through, raising a little girl on his own. What had gone so wrong?

''I'm sorry I kept you up,'' Cassie said quietly.

His gaze faltered. ''I liked you a lot back then, before you didn't want to be held anymore. You were so damned headstrong, just like your—'' He drew in a ragged breath and laid a hand on his chest.

Panic-stricken, Cassie asked, ''Are you okay, Daddy?''

''Just got another pain in my ticker.''

''Should I call a nurse?''

''Nope. No surgery's gonna fix this pain.'' He studied her with rheumy eyes. ''My mama always said you don't leave this earth with things unfinished, so I need to say my piece.'' He sucked in a ragged breath, then let it out slowly. ''I've been hard on you, Cassie girl. But the thing I want you to know is that I'm not good with the emotional stuff, so this is hard on me, but I've gotta do this.''

''You can do it later.''

''I might not have later.'' He scooted up in the bed somewhat and studied her straight on. ''You decided you didn't need me anymore when you were about eleven, so I let you go. I was afraid of being too close to you. When your mama left me, it almost did me in. I couldn't stand the thought of losing you too, so I cut myself off. I know now that

that's why you got into trouble with that boy. But the thing is…'' He looked away once again. "You're the only person in this whole wide world I've got, or at least the only one who counts. It's probably too late to be saying this, and I don't blame you for not forgiving me for being one hard-nosed SOB but I—" He swiped a hand over his eyes and again looked away.

Tears rolled down Cassie's cheek in a steady stream. "I love you, too, Daddy."

A nurse pushed through the door and announced they were ready to transport, interrupting the poignant moment. Cassie brushed away the tears with her jacket sleeve and affected a weak smile aimed at her father, a man she had wanted to hate but hadn't. A man she still loved, despite the heartache. "Now you behave, Coy Allen. No pinching the girls, no trying to sneak a smoke around the oxygen. When you get out, I'll be waiting."

Cassie moved back from the bed, but not before he caught her hand. "You drive a hard bargain, Cass. But I'm just ornery enough to come back around and give you more grief."

She laughed through another rush of tears. "You better." Stepping aside, Cassie allowed the transporters to roll the gurney out the door while she uttered a silent prayer.

Cassie intended to follow but a nurse stopped her in the hall. "You can only go so far, so why don't you take a seat in the waiting room? Dr. Granger will have someone keep you posted."

The room suddenly swayed beneath Cassie's feet and her vision blurred like a worn out picture tube. "I think that's a good idea."

"Mrs. O'Connor, are you okay?"

"I'm feeling a little dizzy."

The woman took her arm and guided her to a chair. "How far along are you? About five months?"

"Almost four. I'm having twins."

"Twins? Come with me."

Cassie rose on shaky legs using the nurse's arm for support. "Where are we going?"

"To the ER."

Nine

"**A**re you having any pain?"

Cassie studied the doctor who seemed much too young to be an experienced obstetrician, and not at all what most would view as a typical physician. His raven hair was pulled low into a ponytail revealing a gold loop in one ear. The faded chambray shirt and jeans, covered by a lab coat, contrasted with his dark skin, as did his arresting topaz eyes. Even his name sounded exotic, Rio Madrid.

He was reportedly taking call for Dr. Anderson, so she had to believe he knew what he was doing. "I'm just a little dizzy, that's all."

"Understandable. Your blood pressure's elevated."

She swallowed around the tight knot of fear in her throat. "Are the babies okay?"

"I have no reason to believe they're not at this

point in time. You don't have any swelling or other symptoms that would indicate otherwise, but I'll need to do more tests to be sure. Have you been hypertensive before?''

''No, never. It's probably stress. My father's having open-heart surgery as we speak.'' *I told my husband to leave me alone.* ''I'm sure as soon as I know he's okay, it will go down.''

''Could be, but you're not going anywhere until I order some blood work and do an ultrasound.''

''I need to get back to—''

''You need to lay low in this bed for a while until we're sure nothing else is wrong.''

Frustrated, afraid, alone, Cassie couldn't stop the onslaught of tears. ''This is great. Just great.''

Dr. Madrid perched on the end of the gurney, a metal chart clutched to his chest. ''Try to calm down if you can. Getting upset isn't good for you or the babies.''

Calm down? ''I'm sorry, Doctor, but I'm concerned about my father and my babies.'' Concerned about Brendan. This would definitely set him on edge, even more so than he had been.

''I've called your husband down from the NICU—''

''No!'' Cassie couldn't face Brendan now. One glimpse of fear in his beautiful green eyes, and she might beg him to come back. She couldn't do that, at least not now. Not until she had more time to think. ''I mean, he doesn't need to worry.''

''He's already on his way.''

''I don't want to see him.''

The doctor's eyes narrowed with perception. ''Problems?''

"You could say that."

He stood and tapped the chart's edge on his open palm. "Okay, that's your call. If it's going to stress you more to have him here, then I'll keep him out until you tell me otherwise."

She swiped at her face with one hand, hating her tears, hating the fact that she wanted Brendan there with all her heart, knowing it would be best to keep him at a distance, at least for now. "Thank you."

"In the meantime, try to relax. I'll get someone in here to take that blood."

Just then a scowling nurse stuck her head inside the open door. "Dr. O'Connor's here, Dr. Madrid. I think you better come talk to him."

"I'll be right there." He patted Cassie's arm. "Rest for a while. I'll handle your husband."

"Good luck."

Cassie got the distinct feeling he would definitely need some luck. But then, so did she. If anything happened to her babies... She refused to think along those lines. Refused to believe that one more terrible thing could happen tonight. Her children would be fine. She would cling to that hope, even if she had lost all hope of ever having Brendan's love.

Brendan's gaze darted from one exam room to the next as he frantically searched the ER corridor for Cassie. When he reached the third cubicle, he was met head-on by some man he didn't recognize.

"Are you Brendan O'Connor?"

Obviously the man recognized him. "Yeah."

The guy was two inches shorter than Brendan, but he managed to block Brendan's path. "I'm Rio Madrid."

Brendan wasn't in the mood to be friendly but took the hand he offered for a shake. "I'm looking for my wife."

"I'm taking care of her."

"Are you an ER doc?"

"Nope. OB."

"Jim Anderson's my wife's OB."

"And I'm Jim Anderson's new partner. Just came onboard yesterday. He left me with call tonight."

The guy looked more biker than doctor. And what the hell kind of name was Rio Madrid? Sounded like a damned resort. "Anderson's familiar with her pregnancy. If there's something wrong—"

"She's slightly hypertensive, but she doesn't have any facial edema, nothing that would indicate pre-eclampsia at this time. I'm waiting for some labs right now. I want to watch her carefully for the next few hours. If all goes well, she can go home to-morrow."

Brendan felt somewhat relieved, but he wouldn't be totally convinced until he could see Cassie. "Where is she?"

He hooked a thumb over his shoulder. "In an exam room. I'll have her transferred onto the L&D floor pretty soon."

"I want to see her."

"Afraid that's not going to happen. She's pretty stressed at the moment."

"Damn straight she is. Her dad's sick."

"She's also requested not to see you."

A spear of anger linked with remorse hurled through Brendan. "She'll change her mind."

"If she does, then I'll let you know."

"You can't stop me from being with her."

"The hell I can't." Madrid slicked a hand over his scalp and nailed Brendan with a severe glare. "Listen, amigo, you're on my turf now, so you will do as I say. Your wife doesn't want to see you at the moment, so you can go back to work or go into the waiting room until the time she gives the okay, *if* she gives the okay. Comprenda?"

Damn him to hell. "I need to be with her."

Madrid's expression turned somewhat sympathetic. "I understand, but I don't want her upset anymore. I'll take good care of her."

Resigned to the fact he wouldn't see Cassie tonight, Brendan turned away, needing to escape, go outside, shout if he had to in order to rid himself of the fury, the fear.

"O'Connor," Madrid called from behind him.

Brendan faced the obstetrician again. "Yeah."

"It's none of my business, but whatever's going on between you two, you better try to fix it quick, for the sake of your wife and children."

Brendan choked down more anger, more regret. The man wasn't telling him anything he didn't already know. But how was he going to fix it if Cassie wouldn't see him?

When Brendan didn't respond, Madrid added, "Losing some of your pride's not as bad as losing someone you love. Seems to me your wife's worth it." Then he headed down the corridor, probably back to Cassie.

A damned stupid thing to be jealous at a time like this, Brendan decided, but he couldn't stop it. He didn't much care for the guy, although he figured a lot of women would. Brendan also acknowledged that Madrid's advice was right on target. He had to get rid of the pride, the fear, tell Cassie everything he was feeling deep inside. Stop shutting her out. But he couldn't do that if she continued to shut him out.

Brendan didn't know what to do, what to think, so he returned to the place where he felt most at home, with the tiny struggling patients who needed him, since his wife no longer believed she did.

After scrubbing in, Brendan paused at the growers and feeders nursery—the place that heralded success—the room that housed babies who had moved from the critical-care area. Millie stood over one crib, conferring with another nurse. She looked up and met his gaze. "Dr. O'Connor, Albers has the unit covered. You didn't have to come back."

"I know, but everything's okay." A huge lie.

"Then Cassie's fine?"

Brendan stepped into the room. "She's got an elevated BP, but it's probably from stress. They're going to keep her overnight. Since I don't intend to leave, I might as well make myself useful."

Millie nodded toward one infant making herself known with an ear-piercing cry. "Maybe you could have a talk with Miss Monica over there. She's not a happy camper. I think she's trying to register a few complaints before she leaves tomorrow. She wants to make sure we don't forget her."

Brendan wouldn't forget the little girl anytime soon. They'd been through a lot together. He'd put her through a lot, yet she had survived. He moved to the baby's crib and laid a hand on her heaving chest. "Hey, kiddo, what's got you so upset tonight?" She stopped bellowing for a moment then commenced crying once again.

"She wants to be held," Millie said. "Her mother isn't due back for a feeding for another half hour. She doesn't like the pacifier."

Brendan glanced at the rubber nipple lying near the infant's tear-damp cheek. "Can't say that I blame her."

"Why don't you do it?"

"Sticking rubber in my mouth isn't at all appetizing."

"I meant hold her. Like a man, not a doctor. Just sit in the rocking chair in the mothers' area and play daddy. Might as well get in some practice."

Brendan stared down at the baby, her fists bunched beneath her chin, her face red from exertion. He could relate to her distress. At the moment he felt like crying, but he wouldn't. He couldn't.

Slipping his arm beneath her tiny body, he brought her to his shoulder. He patted baby Monica's back as he strolled toward the private area reserved for nursing mothers, deserted for the time being, and slipped into one heavy wooden rocker. With his legs stretched out before him, he planted his feet and started the chair in motion.

He took Monica from his shoulder and placed her in the crook of his arm. She stared at him with an unfocused gaze, but quieted somewhat when he began to speak.

"Yeah, I know what you're thinking, there's the guy with all the torture equipment." Her bottom lip puckered as if she wanted to cry again. "Hey, I promise I don't have one needle or tube on me. You can frisk me if you want."

She let loose a lingering sob but continued to gaze at him, as if she did recognize him. Her eyes drifted shut as Brendan continued to rock in a slow, steady rhythm. Shifting her once again to his shoulder, he leaned his head back and closed his eyes, relishing the feel of the tiny miracle in his arms. She smelled clean, baby-fresh, innocent, felt warm against him, welcome.

His thoughts whirled back to another time, another place, another child. A child so small he could have fit in the palm of Brendan's hand. A child with dark hair much like his own. A child he had only been able to hold deep within his heart.

Brendan tried to imagine what it would have been like to hold his own son, at least for a little while. If only he had been given the opportunity to say goodbye.

He thought about Cassie then, about how much she had brought to his life, how scared he had been when he had learned she was sick. He was still scared, more than he'd ever been in his adult life. More than he had been the night he'd lost his only child. If anything happened to Cassie, he couldn't live with himself. He couldn't imagine living without her.

Truth was, his fear stemmed from that loss more than the prospect of losing his unborn children, although that was something he didn't want to cope with again. But without Cassie, nothing made any sense. Nothing he did at work would mean as much without her guidance, her friendship, her laughter...her love.

Even with the precious gift in his arms, Brendan felt completely alone, bereft. The bittersweet emotions swamped him, made him hurt desperately, made him claim them for the first time in thirteen long years. The tears slipped from the corners of his eyes and he welcomed them, let them fall and roll back from his face as he gave in to the silent mourning.

In the silence of the nursery, the occasional baby cry as a backdrop, Brendan grieved for his lost child. Grieved the prospective loss of Cassie. He didn't know what to do, where to turn. Cassie had become his life, although he'd been too stupid to acknowledge that, too proud and afraid to let her know how much she meant to him. And now it might be too late.

The sound of voices coming from nearby caused Brendan to swipe a hand over the moisture on his face. The baby shifted in his arms and released a tiny whimper of protest.

"Dr. O'Connor?"

Brendan looked up to see Mrs. Neely near the partition separating the area from the nursery, a pleasant yet surprised smile on her face.

"Must be feeding time," Brendan said.

"Yes, it is." Mrs. Neely approached him slowly. "The nurse said Monica's been fussy."

Brendan sent her a half smile, feeling self-conscious. "I think she just wants some company." So did he, from his wife.

"You look very natural holding her," Mrs. Neely said. "Millie told me you're getting in some practice being a father."

Leave it to Millie to make that announcement. "Yeah. Hope you don't mind."

"Not at all. And congratulations." She took another step forward. "Will this be your first child?"

Slowly Brendan stood and placed the baby in her mother's arms. For all intents and purposes, it was a first in some ways. His first babies with Cassie, his first opportunity to be a real father, his first attempt at trying to be a good husband, if only Cassie gave him another chance.

But there was still another child that he rarely spoke of. A child that still lived deeply engrained in his memory, in his heart. He'd kept those memories, those bittersweet emotions, hidden behind a wall of remorse, of guilt. The dam broke, crumbling that wall, and he acknowledged what he had failed to acknowledge up to this point in his life.

"No, it isn't my first. I lost a child some years ago. A son, when he was only a few hours old."

Mrs. Neely gave him a sympathetic look, one of understanding. "I'm sorry to hear that. I suppose there's nothing worse. But I'm confident everything will turn out well for you this time, as it has for us."

Brendan was beginning to feel that might be a possibility, at least where his unborn children were concerned. "I hope so."

She nodded toward the sleeping baby, lying content in her mother's arms. "Just look at this little one. She's proof that miracles do happen. You only have to believe."

"God knows I see it happen every day." Something he should consider more often—the miracles, not the failures. He vowed to do that from this point forward.

Mrs. Neely's smile was kind, thoughtful. "And you have a hand in that, too, helping those babies get well. What a wonderful gift. So remember your lost child, but don't forget you'll have your own miracle soon. Don't ever forget the living."

In that moment Brendan realized he was finally ready to say goodbye to his son.

He would never forget him, but he could move on and look toward the future. A future that would mean nothing without Cassie in it. And dammit, he was going to make certain that she was a part of his life. He wasn't sure exactly how he was going to do that, but he was determined to try. Determined to use every trick in the book to make her understand how much she meant to him. How much he loved her.

Mrs. Neely took the chair next to the one he had occupied. Brendan decided to leave then, give her some privacy, but she stopped him before he could make a quick exit. "Dr. O'Connor, when we take her home tomorrow, is there something special I should do?"

Aside from the monitor that would accompany her, the standard instructions that would be covered at the time of dismissal, Brendan could think of only one thing. "Just take her home and love her, Mrs. Neely."

Her mother's smile expanded with joy. "That I can do. And thank you so much. We'll never be able to repay you for what you've done."

"No payment necessary. Just send me a picture now and then for my collection." The same thing he told all concerned parents, and his collection was growing larger every day. But he wouldn't be satisfied until he had photos of his own children in that scrapbook, alongside one of his beautiful wife.

Brendan studied the man's face illuminated by the harsh glare in the Cardiac Care Unit. He tried to see some resemblance to Cassie in Coy Allen, but he didn't find any, until the man opened his eyes. They were dark, like Cassie's, but not nearly as wise.

"Who are you?" His voice came out in a grinding croak.

"Brendan O'Connor, Cassie's husband."

"You a heart doctor?"

"No. I take care of sick babies."

"Oh." He started to drift off again, then his eyes snapped open. "Where's my daughter?"

Brendan thought it wise not to reveal that Cassie was up on the labor floor in a hospital bed. "She's sleeping. She needs some rest."

"Yeah. She's so hardheaded I'm surprised..." He licked his dry lips. "I expected to see her down here, telling me what to do."

"That's why I'm here, to check on you, I mean. Let her know how you're doing. Looks like you're doing pretty well."

"Just glad to be awake. Glad to be alive."

Brendan glanced at the cardiac monitor, noting everything looked good. "Well, you've made it through the toughest part. Now you need to focus on recovering."

"You sound like Cassie."

Brendan realized she had taught him a lot. "Just trying to help out. Cassie needs you."

"She has you now."

If only she still wanted him, Brendan thought. "She's not going to desert you."

The man's eyes looked misty. "Nope. She never has, and God only knows why she's put up with me. But I'm gonna be better to her when I get out of here."

"I'm sure you will." Brendan glanced at the exit. "I've got to go now. Have them page me if you need anything. I'm sure Cassie will be in to see you when she can."

Coy's eyes drifted shut then opened once again. "Hey, Doc, one more thing before you leave."

"Sure."

"Be good to my daughter. You know, her mama left when Cassie was a baby. And me being the way I am, she's never had it easy." He cleared his throat. "What I'm trying to say is love her good and long. She deserves that. She's a good kid."

An exceptional woman, Brendan decided, one who did deserve the best. "I'm going to try." If Cassie would let him. "I'll let you get some sleep now. Take it easy."

Coy closed his eyes once again and muttered something about a bicycle. Brendan figured he probably wouldn't even remember their conversation, but hopefully there would be time later to get acquainted with his father-in-law.

First he had to get reacquainted with his wife, start over, make her understand that they belonged together.

In order to do that, he had to prove to her that he wanted their marriage to work. He'd have to plan carefully, beginning tonight.

"How are you feeling, Mrs. O'Connor?"

Cassie woke to the sound of Dr. Madrid's voice. She wanted to go back to sleep, since she'd barely dozed off only a few hours before, but she clawed her way back into wakefulness to face the new day, alone. "I'm okay, I guess."

"Your blood pressure's leveled off, which leads me to believe it was probably only stress."

Suddenly Cassie remembered the events leading up to her arrival on the labor and delivery unit. "How's my father?"

"He's doing okay, according to your husband."

"My husband?"

"Yeah. He told me to tell you that your dad made it through the surgery fine and was talking when he went to see him. He's in the Cardiac Intensive Care Unit and he's stable."

"Brendan's been to see him?"

"Looks that way."

Cassie glanced away from the doctor's assessing eyes. "Is Brendan here?"

Dr. Madrid set the chart on the rolling lap table near the bed. "He was earlier." He nodded toward a sack resting on the chair. "He brought you some clothes, then headed out."

"Did he say where he was going?"

"Yeah. He said something about having to move some things, and he wanted me to tell you he's sorry. I told him to stick around, tell you himself, but he said he had to go."

Cassie's heart took a nosedive. "I guess he's not coming back, then."

"Maybe he's waiting for you to ask him to come back."

Oh, how she wanted to, but Brendan had obviously decided to move on, exactly what she'd asked him to do. Maybe she could stop him, tell him she'd changed her mind.

Cassie straightened in the bed and battled the threatening tears. "When can I leave here?"

Rio Madrid started toward the door. "I want you to stay until this evening. Get some rest. If your pressure remains stable, then I'll let you go home."

Cassie hated the thought of remaining one more minute in the hospital bed, but she hated even more the prospect of returning to an empty house without her husband. "I can't leave any earlier?"

"Tell you what, I'll check on you right after lunch. Then we'll see."

By then it might be too late, but she had no choice. She needed to make sure everything was okay with the pregnancy, her babies. After today they might be all she'd have left of Brendan, aside from the memories.

No longer able to hold back the tears, Cassie turned her face away and stared out the window.

"Con amor hay siempre sitio para el perdón."

Cassie swiped at her eyes and turned back to Rio Madrid. "Beg pardon?"

He smiled. "It's something my mother always told me. With love there is always room for forgiveness. Just something to think about." With that he was out the door.

Cassie did think on his words for a long moment. Her father hadn't forgiven her mother, but he had attempted to make amends with Cassie. Cassie was more than ready to forgive her dad, forget the past, start anew. She would be willing to do the same for Brendan, if she could be assured that someday he might love her. She'd be willing to work harder, tell him how much she loved him, how badly she hated the thought of living without him. How she'd made a mistake by asking him to go. Yet it looked as though she wouldn't get that chance. Not now, anyway.

Maybe not ever.

"Out of that bed, Cassie O'Connor. Time's awastin'."

Cassie looked up from the magazine she'd been attempting to read to find Michelle Kempner standing at the hospital door. "What are you doing here?"

Michelle walked to the end of the bed and smiled. "I'm here to spring you. Dr. Madrid said you can go home, and I'm in charge of taking you there."

Sitting up, Cassie draped her legs over the end of the bed. "How did you come by that honor?"

Michelle looked away. "Brendan called me and told me what happened with your dad, about your blood pressure. He asked me if I'd drive you home."

Cassie swallowed around the lump in her throat. "I guess I thought maybe he'd offer to do that."

Michelle turned her attention back to Cassie. "He had some things to do, or so he told me."

"Move out of my house, I imagine," Cassie muttered.

"Why do you think that?"

Cassie blew out a ragged breath. "Because I asked him to, that's why."

Michelle frowned. "How did that happen?"

"Because at the time it seemed like a good idea." Cassie sighed. "It's a long story, Michelle."

Michelle held up a hand. "I understand if you don't want to talk about it now. You've been through enough. Is there something I can do?"

Shaking her head, Cassie said, "No, I don't think there's anything anyone can do."

"I don't believe that. You and Brendan are made for each other. When I talked to him earlier, he sounded terrible. I doubt he wants this marriage to end any more than you do."

"If that's true, then why isn't he here?"

"Do you think maybe it's because he believes you don't want him here?"

Cassie knew Michelle was right. They were both at odds over what to say. Brendan had only done what she'd asked of him. She couldn't blame him. "You're right. I told Dr. Madrid that I didn't want to see him. Now I've totally screwed everything up."

"Maybe not, Cassie. There's still time. If you hurry and get dressed, maybe you'll catch him at home before he leaves."

Filled with determination, and more energy than she'd had in days, Cassie slipped out of the bed and headed for the bag of clothes Brendan had brought her. "You're right. Go get the car and bring it out front. I'll get dressed."

Michelle grinned. "That's the spirit. I'll meet you downstairs."

Cassie suddenly remembered her father. Now she was really torn between checking on him before she left and hurrying home to see if she could stop Brendan from leaving. More than likely, Brendan was already gone.

"Actually, Michelle, I need to see about my dad before I leave."

"Okay. Take your time. I'll just hang out at the exit until I see the whites of your eyes."

After Michelle left, Cassie made quick work dressing and signed the dismissal forms one nurse brought to her. Just when she was about to fold her copy of the paper and put it away, she noted the final instructions from Dr. Madrid. ''Patient may return to work in two days and may resume normal activities with emphasis on those that aid in relieving stress, including lovemaking.''

Cassie folded the paper and smiled to herself. Dr. Madrid was quite a character. If only she believed that she'd have the opportunity to follow his instructions.

Simply too much to wish for.

Ten

The closer they got to the house, the more Cassie's anxiety grew. In her heart of hearts she knew she wouldn't find Brendan there. He'd had plenty of time to move his things, get out of her life.

Earlier she'd briefly visited her father, who was in and out of consciousness, then stopped by her office and paged Brendan. Millie had returned the call, stating that Brendan was scheduled to be off work for three days, didn't she know?

Cassie had lied and said of course, she knew, she thought maybe he'd stopped back by the unit before they left for home. Millie allowed as how she hadn't seen him since the night before, inquired about Cassie's health, then told her to take care of herself. After Cassie had hung up, she'd left the hospital with a heavy heart and an abject sadness like she'd never known before.

The sun had already set when Michelle pulled her car up to the curb. Cassie retrieved her bag from the back seat and hesitated. She dreaded the thought of going into the empty house alone. "Do you want to come in for a minute?" she asked.

Michelle put the car in gear but left it running. "First of all, Nick's waiting for me. Second, three's a crowd."

"The cat won't care, Michelle," Cassie said, a dumb attempt at humor when she wanted nothing more than to cry. "You wouldn't have to stay long. Just have one cup of tea, then you can be on your way."

Michelle nodded toward the driveway. "Forgive me if I'm mistaken, but isn't that Brendan's car?"

Cassie's gaze snapped toward the sedan parked in front of hers. Evidently he'd managed to bring her car home, and obviously he was still there.

The atmosphere was suddenly incredibly warm, stifling, without oxygen. "Yes, it's his car."

"Then it looks to me like you won't be alone."

Cassie didn't move, couldn't move. She felt frozen with dread. "I don't think I can face him."

"Sure you can," Michelle said firmly. "Now's your chance. You two need to talk."

"What if he doesn't want to talk?"

"My guess is he's been waiting for you to come home."

If only Cassie could believe he was waiting for her, instead of thinking he probably hadn't finished packing his stuff. Regardless, she couldn't run away. She had to face him, face what came next, if only to say goodbye.

Inhaling a cleansing breath, Cassie opened the

door and slid out. She leaned back into the car and tried to smile. "Thanks, Michelle. Wish me luck."

Michelle returned her smile. "You don't need to rely on luck, Cassie. You just need to rely on your love. Call me in the morning."

Cassie promised she would, knowing she'd probably need a shoulder to cry on, then headed toward the front door on wooden legs. She turned the knob to find it open, thankfully, since she didn't have her keys. With Brendan not having to let her in, she had a little more time to prepare.

Once inside, she didn't see Brendan anywhere. She did see a few large boxes stacked in the dining room. As suspected, she'd caught him in the middle of moving, and her heart began to ache with that knowledge. How stupid that she'd thought maybe he'd changed his mind.

Dropping the sack containing her clothes onto the sofa, she trudged, weary and heartsick, into the kitchen to regroup. Mister greeted her, twining in and out of her legs and mewling incessantly. At least someone missed her. She picked up the cat and held him close to her chest, rubbing her cheek back and forth over his soft fur, holding back the tears with sheer will. She didn't want to cry. Not until after he left.

"How are you feeling?"

Slowly Cassie turned to the sound of the deep voice, a voice that could make her tremble, make her want, with only a few simple words.

Brendan stood in the doorway to the hall dressed in a T-shirt and jeans, his eyes weary and red-rimmed. He looked exhausted but surprisingly calm.

Why shouldn't he be, Cassie thought. She had given him the out he'd wanted.

Cassie put the cat down and crossed her arms over her chest. "I'm fine." Her tone was harsher than she'd intended, but it was best to hide her sadness with detachment, even anger.

A long silence stretched between them as Cassie tried to decide what to say. What could she say? That she didn't want him to go? That she loved him and wanted to start over? Her pride prevented her from doing that. She would let him have his say, then be done with it. "Brendan, I—"

"Don't say anything yet, Cassie." He held out his hand to her. "I want to show you something first."

Cassie took his hand. It felt strong and warm, yet she felt a soul-deep chill, confused when he led her down the hall. He stopped at the guest room door before turning to her once again.

"Close your eyes," he said.

Curious, Cassie complied. Brendan opened the door, clasped her shoulders and guided her inside the room.

"Okay," he said. "Open them."

Cassie did, slowly, and gasped over the sight. Where before there had only been functional white walls, the room was now decorated in bright blues and greens and reds. The ceiling was bordered with multicolored hot-air balloons piloted by various animals, bears and giraffes and the like. Against one wall, two matching cribs formed a vee in the corner, both containing tiny comforters that complemented the border along with corresponding mobiles. The day bed was still present, moved to the opposite wall and covered in a royal blue spread, two oak rocking chairs set next to it.

Cassie's hand drifted to her chest at the moment tears drifted down her cheeks. "Oh, Brendan. It's beautiful."

"Are you sure? We can change it if you want."

She walked to one crib and ran her fingertips along the railing. "No, it's perfect." She faced him again. "How did you get this done in one day?"

Brendan took a seat on the edge of the day bed. "I started early this morning moving furniture until the shops opened. Then Nick came by and helped me put the beds together and hang the border. Michelle helped some, too. That's when I asked her to pick you up."

"So, she knew about this all along?"

"Yeah, but she promised to keep it a secret."

"That she did." Cassie swiped at her face and took a couple of steps forward. "Did Michelle help you pick out the bedding?"

His smile came halfway with a hint of pride. "No. I did that myself." Patting the bed, he said, "Come here."

Cassie slowly moved to the bed and sat on the edge, maintaining some distance between them when all she really wanted to do was throw herself into his arms. But this gesture of putting together a nursery, although wonderful, was for their babies. It had nothing to do with their relationship beyond sharing the parenting of two children.

Brendan streaked both hands over his face. "Do you remember the day we met?"

Caught off balance, Cassie could only nod though she remembered every detail.

"I remember it well," he continued. "I came in the cafeteria for lunch and I saw you across the room. You had grape juice down the front of your blouse. I think someone had run into you."

Cassie smiled through her tears. "It was a doctor."

"Yeah, and I handed you my napkin, and you said something about avoiding wearing white except when you played tennis."

"And then you told me you played, and we had our first match the next night."

"After that we had a beer at Malone's, and you asked me if I had the opportunity to do one thing I'd never done before, what would it be. I told you—"

"Get a good night's sleep."

Brendan's grin expanded, lighting up his beautiful green eyes, much as they had that first day they'd met. The day she had fallen hopelessly in love with him. "You told me you wanted to ride in a hot-air balloon." He gestured toward the miniature balloons comprising the mobile. "That's why I decided on this theme."

Cassie recalled telling him that over their first beer, recalled watching him talk that night, thinking how gorgeous he was, how gentle he seemed, although even then she'd sensed his wounds ran deep. "I can't believe you remembered."

"I remember a lot of things about you. I remember your smile, how much I enjoyed being around you from that first night. Hell, that first minute. I remember how much I wanted you in every way."

Cassie's eyes widened. "You did?"

His laugh was cynical. "Yeah. Really bad. But I

recognized right away you were different from most women I'd known before, and I really needed a friend at the time, not a lover. But I can't tell you how many times I wanted to take you home with me, make love to you, to hell with friendship. I didn't because I was afraid I'd mess everything up."

Cassie looked away, wondering where this was all leading. Leading to an admission that by becoming lovers, they had ruined any chance of a deeper relationship? His lead-in to goodbye? "I guess I always thought that friendship was a great foundation for a deeper relationship."

"It is," he admitted. "I've never known that before you. Never had many women friends, I guess. This time I wanted more. I still want more."

Cassie met his gaze. "What are you saying?"

He took her hands into his, his expression reflecting anxiety and concern. "Last night, when I found out you were sick, it almost killed me."

She squeezed his hands. "Our babies are fine, Brendan."

"It wasn't only the twins. It was the thought that something might happen to you. That I might not have you in my life anymore. I want these babies, Cassie, but if I lost you...well..."

He studied the ceiling for a moment before bringing his eyes, darkened by emotion, back to her. "I can't count the times we talked about what we wanted, skirting the real issues. The things that are important. And having you as my wife is the most important thing to me. So I'm asking you now, Cassie, is there a chance we can try again?"

Oh, how she wanted to scream yes. How she wanted to hold him, tell him nothing would make her happier, but she still needed to let him know exactly how she felt, and exactly what she expected. "I love you, Brendan. I have for months. That's why this has been so difficult. I want to try and make it work, but I have to know that you do care for me beyond friendship. That I'm not going to continue to be invisible in your life. I've lived that way before, and I can't do it again."

He braced her cheeks in his palms and leaned his forehead against hers. "When I heard that door open tonight, it took everything in me not to hit my knees and beg you to let me stay. I don't have any pride left, Cassie. But I do know one thing for sure." He gently kissed her forehead and leveled his soulful green eyes on her. "I'm not ashamed to admit that if you make me leave, I won't go quietly. I'll be on your doorstep every day pleading my case. I'm also not ashamed to say that I love you more than I ever thought I could love anyone. Not just as a friend. As a lover and my wife."

She couldn't stifle the sob, the tears of joy, the feelings of pure, undisguised love for this man who had given her not only the prospect of a family, but the promise of a future. "I love you, too, Brendan. So much."

"Then you want me to stay?"

"Yes. As long as it's forever."

"Forever you have."

He kissed her then, a kiss full of the love he'd declared so sweetly, filling Cassie's heart with contentment, with the realization that she had finally found home in his arms.

Filled with joy, with desire intermingled with need, Cassie pulled him back on the bed in her arms.

Brendan groaned, then broke the kiss but didn't let her go. "I'm about to lose it here, Cassie, but I'm a mess. I need a shower."

Cassie grinned. "So do I."

"Well, we might as well conserve some water since I spent a hefty amount of money today on our kids."

"I imagine it's only the beginning."

"I imagine you're right." His expression went serious once again. "Are you sure you're feeling okay?"

"Couldn't be better."

"I really want to make love to you, but only if you're feeling up to it."

"Oh, I am." She squirmed against him. "And so are you."

He returned her smile. "I sure as hell can't argue that."

"First, there's something I need to show you that should put your mind at ease." She pulled him up from the bed and took him to the living room. Rifling through the sack, she withdrew the dismissal papers and showed him Rio Madrid's directive. "It seems to me that the doctor has given us permission to resume normal activities."

A devious grin appeared on Brendan's face. "To be honest, I asked him about this very thing, just in case. He told me to do what I had to do to keep you in bed for the next two days."

Cassie yanked the paper from his grasp, rolled it up and slapped Brendan playfully on the arm with it. "Pretty optimistic, I'd say, Dr. O'Connor."

"Pretty smart, if you ask me."

Scooping her up into his arms, he carried her into

the bathroom. Without formality they shed their clothes and entered the shower together, taking turns washing each other, touching each other, building the tension until neither could hold out any longer.

They made haste drying off, unable to keep their hands to themselves long enough to have much success. Giving up, Brendan once again gathered Cassie into his arms and took her to the bed. They sank down together, blanketed only in love.

Brendan left no part of Cassie untouched, loving her thoroughly with his hands, his mouth, and she did the same. They finally came together with a long sigh. Brendan tempered his movements, gently, slowly, building a steady tempo as he moved inside Cassie's body, touching her soul-deep with whispered words of love.

Cassie slipped away first, fell headlong into pleasure. Brendan followed soon after, calling her name on a harsh whisper.

In the aftermath they held on to each other in silence, until Brendan spoke again. "I think I need to thank that guy."

Cassie raised her head from Brendan's chest. "Dr. Madrid?"

"No. The one that made you spill the grape juice."

"He's a neuro doctor. Lane somebody."

"Billings. The cowboy neurosurgeon."

"Yeah, that's him." Cassie kissed his cheek. "If I see him, I'll be sure to thank him."

"No way," Brendan growled. "He's single. I don't want him thinking that my wife might be propositioning him."

Cassie laughed. "Are you jealous, Dr. O'Connor?"

"Yeah. As a matter of fact, I am."

"Well, at least we'll have a story to tell our children."

Brendan tightened his hold on her. "Yeah, who would've thought destiny would come in the form of grape juice."

Destiny.

Cassie accepted that fate had played a part in their relationship. But more important, destiny had taken a back seat to love. A love that was destined to see them through the birth of their children and a marriage that would be as strong as the man who held her so closely.

"I love you, Brendan," she said, so happy that she could finally voice her feelings out loud.

"I love you, too, babe." He raised himself up on one elbow and grinned. "Now what do you say we go get a bite to eat? You're going to need your strength."

Cassie gave him her best smile. "Sounds like a great idea. I'm having a craving."

"Let me guess. Mocha almond fudge ice cream."

"No. Grape juice."

Brendan released a deep, rich laugh that came from low in his chest, from the heart. Cassie delighted in the sound, thrilled in the fact Brendan was back, only better this time. At peace. Relaxed. In love...with her.

"It's good to hear you laugh again, Dr. O'Connor."

"It feels good to laugh. Good to have a reason to laugh. You make me glad to be alive."

Cassie draped her arms around his neck and brought him back down into her arms to hold him tightly, thankful for her blessings, for finally reaching the man beneath the doctor. "You make me happy, too. It's all anyone could hope to give someone they love."

"You've given me more than I ever imagined." He lowered his head to her abdomen and brushed a kiss across the place that sheltered their beloved babies. "This is the greatest gift of all."

Epilogue

Brendan O'Connor counted fingers, counted toes and counted his blessings.

His squirming daughter rested across her mother's belly still housing her sibling. She let it be known with a piercing cry, without question, that she was none too happy to be facing the harsh light of the delivery suite. Brendan reveled in the sound, a solid hale and hearty cry that grew in volume when Millie carried her away to the nearby warming crib.

He wrestled with the urge to join the neonatology team overseeing his baby girl. He'd insisted on their presence even though Cassie was less than two weeks from term. His daughter was in good hands, and Cassie needed him now since they still awaited the birth of the second twin.

"She's six pounds, three ounces," Millie called out. "Nineteen inches long, great Apgar scores."

Damn good news, Brendan thought. But it wasn't over yet. One down, still one to go.

Brendan reclaimed his place at Cassie's side. The signs of exertion showed in her face and her damp, furrowed brow. He stroked her hair and told her, "Come on, babe. Hang in there. You're almost done."

"I know," she said on a broken breath. "And I think this is it."

"Don't push, Cassie," Anderson commanded. "This one's anterior presentation."

Cassie released a frustrated moan and Brendan tried not to panic. Babies presented anterior every day without any complications. They had gotten this far; he couldn't even consider that something might go wrong now.

"What's happening, Brendan?" Cassie asked, fear in her voice as she tried to breathe through the contraction.

"The baby's turned faceup," Brendan said, forcing a calm tone. "It might take a little longer."

"Not likely," Anderson announced. "I've got this one turned, and we're ready to go."

"A sign of intelligence," Rio Madrid said. He'd come along to assist Jim Anderson since he would soon be taking over his practice. "This one wants to see who's about to catch him, or her."

Brendan was glad that he and Cassie had chosen to be surprised about their babies' genders. It really didn't matter to Brendan if he ended up with two girls, as long as they were both healthy. He sent up a silent prayer that that would be the case.

"One more push, Cassie," Anderson said.

With her chin tucked to her chest, Brendan bracing her legs, Cassie bore down once more. Brendan was amazed at her strength, considering she had been pushing for over an hour. Amazed at how well she had handled twelve hours of labor.

"It's a boy," Madrid proclaimed with a grin.

Anderson placed the baby on Cassie's belly where his sister had lain a few moments before. A few seconds of silence ticked off before he puckered up, opened his eyes and screamed bloody murder. Brendan laughed with relief while Cassie laid a hand on the baby's head. Cutting the cord, Brendan severed mother and child physically and created a bond between parents and child that could never be broken.

Another nurse whisked the baby away to the second warmer to be checked out by the team while Brendan waited anxiously for the verdict. His son looked to be in great shape, but he knew all too well that sometimes looks could be deceptive.

"This one weighs almost seven pounds. Twenty inches long, and he has a big head. No doubt he'll be a doctor, too." Millie turned toward Brendan with a smirk and released her trademark, sandpaper laugh. "Good God, Dr. O'Connor. What have you been feeding your wife? Whole hams? These two are as big as singletons."

Brendan pushed Cassie's damp hair away from her forehead and sent her a teasing grin. "She ate anything that would sit still long enough."

"Don't listen to him, Millie." Cassie frowned at Brendan. "I might have just given birth, but I'm not too weak to slug you."

"I'd rather you kiss me."

"That I can do."

Brendan brushed a soft kiss over her lips, then another.

After studying him a long moment, Cassie said, "Go."

"You want me to leave? After the great job I did coaching you through this whole ordeal?"

She smiled and touched his face. "I mean go over there and check on your children. I know you want to."

Brendan did want to, but he wouldn't. Not today. "Right now I'm the dad, not the doctor."

"Just what I thought."

Millie's declaration caused Brendan's head to snap around toward the dual cribs. "What's wrong?"

"Not a thing, Doc. And that's my point. You don't need us. If these kiddos were any healthier, you would've had to hire a crane to get Cassie out of the car."

Everyone laughed then, even Brendan. But he still wasn't completely satisfied. "Are you sure everything's okay?"

"A-okay," Millie said. "No breathing problems. Everything's working. Your son just baptized me but good."

"You probably deserved it, Millie Beth," Brendan said, followed by another laugh.

Millie faced Brendan with a hand on her hip. "So get over here, daddy, and take these babies to meet their mama."

"My pleasure." After giving Cassie another kiss, Brendan walked to the first warmer holding his daughter. Another nurse had wrapped her in a pink-and-yellow blanket, a matching pink stocking cap

covering her dark hair. She picked up the baby and
handed her to Brendan. He could only stare with
awe at his daughter's miniature features much like
her mother's, her upturned nose, the single dimple
at the corner of her mouth exactly like his, the one
he'd inherited from his own mother. He couldn't
wait for his parents to arrive the next morning. He
had no doubt they would love their grandchildren as
much as they loved Cassie, and him.

"Don't forget this little man," Millie said.

Brendan already felt overwhelmed simply holding
his daughter. "Maybe I should hand this one off
first."

Millie picked up the blue bundle and held it toward him. "You might as well get used to two at a
time."

"Yeah, you're right."

"I always am."

Moving to the next warmer, Brendan allowed
Millie to place his son in the crook of his other arm.

His son.

The memories niggled at his brain, memories of
another little boy. Conflicting emotions stirred
within him, sadness mixed with joy. The joy took
precedence over the regret this time. Brendan had
no trouble putting everything in perspective now,
thanks to this miracle. Thanks to his wife.

The child in his arms, staring up at him with unfocused dark-blue eyes, dark hair that matched his
sister's, served as a reminder that with love and
hope, a few prayers on the side, so much was possible. Brendan's heart opened up and embraced all
three of his children. He would never forget his first

little boy, yet he chose to heed the advice Mrs.
Neely had given him six months ago.

Don't ever forget the living.

And he wouldn't, nor would he forget his good
fortune in finding someone so special to share in this
special moment—his wonderful wife.

"Can I have my turn now, Dr. Dad?" Cassie
asked.

With the babies in tow, Brendan slipped back
onto the stool beside the bed while the neonatal crew
filtered out, expressing congratulations as they went.
He handed his son off to Cassie first and held tight
to his daughter. If he didn't know better, he'd swear
she smiled at him. Already plotting against her dad,
he suspected. Already wrapping his heart around her
tiny finger.

"Guess I could go get your dad now," Brendan
said. "He's pacing a hole in the hall carpet."

"In a little while." Cassie reached over and took
their little girl's hand into hers. "We have to decide
on names."

"Rio's something you might want to consider,"
Madrid said with a grin as he strolled to the bedside.

Brendan nixed that idea immediately. He still
thought the guy's name sounded like it belonged in
the Mexican Riviera. "We're thinking Andrew."

"Ah," Rio said. "And your daughter?"

"Alexandra, after Brendan's grandmother," Cassie added.

Rio rubbed his chin. "Good strong names. You're
lucky they were born under a full moon." He nodded toward the window where a huge yellow moon
shone bright on the night horizon.

"Yeah, a lot of babies are born during full moons." How well Brendan knew that to be true.

"My mother believed that denotes good fortune." Madrid laid his hand first on one baby's forehead, then the other. "I believe she was right. You're both lucky to have these two. Lucky to have each other." With that he was gone.

Dr. Anderson soon exited after more good wishes, leaving only Cassie and Brendan alone with their children for the time being.

"Alex and Andrew," Brendan said, testing the sound, and liking what he heard.

"Lexie and Drew."

"So you say."

"So I know."

"Perfect," Brendan said.

Cassie looked at their children and smiled a mother's smile. "These two are perfect."

Brendan couldn't agree more, and for that he would forever be grateful. He laid his daughter in Cassie's arm and took his son from her. "We couldn't have done any better."

Cassie touched his face lovingly. "You know something? I've decided there's a reason why you've been given two children." She nodded toward Andrew. "I know he'll never replace your other son, but I believe you've been twice blessed because of all the good you've done."

In that moment Brendan couldn't have loved his wife more. "Three times blessed, counting you."

Cassie's dark eyes misted. "I love you, Brendan."

"I love you, too, Cassie. Without you, this wouldn't be possible."

Without her, his work wouldn't have as much meaning. Without her, the losses would be more painful, the victories less sweet. Without Cassie, this moment would never have come, and he would never have known such serenity.

But tonight he felt an indescribable peace, an abiding love, and he owed it all to his lover, his wife, the mother of his children.

His very best friend.

*   *   *   *   *

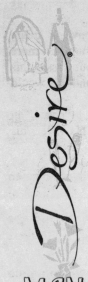

April 2002
MR. TEMPTATION
#1430 by Cait London

HEARTBREAKERS

Don't miss the first book in
Cait London's sensual new
miniseries featuring to-die-for
heroes and the women they love.

May 2002
HIS MAJESTY, M.D.
#1435 by Leanne Banks

Leanne Banks continues
her exciting miniseries about
a royal family faced with the
ultimate temptation—love.

June 2002
A COWBOY'S PURSUIT
#1441 by Anne McAllister

Bestselling author
Anne McAllister's
sexy cowboy heroes
are determined to win
the hearts of the women
they've chosen.

MAN OF THE MONTH

Some men are made for lovin'—and you're sure to love
these three upcoming men of the month!

Available at your favorite retail outlet.

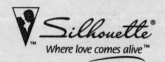

magazine

♥──────────────────────────── **quizzes**

Is he the one? What kind of lover are you? Visit the **Quizzes**
area to find out!

♥──────────────────── **recipes for romance**

Get scrumptious meal ideas with our **Recipes for Romance**.

♥──────────────────── **romantic movies**

Peek at the **Romantic Movies** area to find Top 10 Flicks
about First Love, ten Supersexy Movies, and more.

♥──────────────────────── **royal romance**

Get the latest scoop on your favorite royals in **Royal Romance**.

♥──────────────────────────────── **games**

Check out the **Games** pages to find a ton of interactive
romantic fun!

♥──────────────────── **romantic travel**

In need of a romantic rendezvous? Visit the **Romantic Travel**
section for articles and guides.

♥──────────────────────── **lovescopes**

Are you two compatible? Click your way to the **Lovescopes**
area to find out now!

♥ Silhouette® —

where love comes alive—online...

SINTMAG

*Silhouette presents an exciting
new continuity series:*

**When a royal family rolls out the red carpet
for love, power and deception, will their
lives change forever?**

The saga begins in April 2002 with:

The Princess Is Pregnant!

by Laurie Paige (SE #1459)

**May: THE PRINCESS AND THE DUKE by Allison Leigh
(SE #1465)**

**June: ROYAL PROTOCOL by Christine Flynn
(SE #1471)**

Be sure to catch all nine Crown and Glory stories: the first three appear in
Silhouette Special Edition, the next three continue in Silhouette Romance
and the saga concludes with three books in Silhouette Desire.

————————————

**And be sure not to miss more royal stories,
from Silhouette Intimate Moments'**

Romancing
the Crown,

running January through December.

Where love comes alive™

*Available at
your favorite
retail outlet.*

Visit Silhouette at www.eHarlequin.com   SSECAG

Silhouette® Desire®

presents

DYNASTIES: THE CONNELLYS

A brand-new miniseries about the Connellys of Chicago,
a wealthy, powerful American family tied by blood to the
royal family of the island kingdom of Altaria.
They're wealthy, powerful and rocked by
scandal, betrayal…and passion!

Look for a whole year of glamorous and
utterly romantic tales in 2002:

January: **TALL, DARK & ROYAL** by Leanne Banks

February: **MATERNALLY YOURS** by Kathie DeNosky

March: **THE SHEIKH TAKES A BRIDE** by Caroline Cross

April: **THE SEAL'S SURRENDER** by Maureen Child

May: **PLAIN JANE & DOCTOR DAD** by Kate Little

June: **AND THE WINNER GETS…MARRIED!** by Metsy Hingle

July: **THE ROYAL & THE RUNAWAY BRIDE** by Kathryn Jensen

August: **HIS E-MAIL ORDER WIFE** by Kristi Gold

September: **THE SECRET BABY BOND** by Cindy Gerard

October: **CINDERELLA'S CONVENIENT HUSBAND**
by Katherine Garbera

November: **EXPECTING…AND IN DANGER** by Eileen Wilks

December: **CHEROKEE MARRIAGE DARE**
by Sheri WhiteFeather

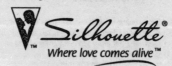

Silhouette®
Where love comes alive™